Juicy
A Twilight Teahouse Story

TJ Michaels

JUICY (*TWILIGHT TEAHOUSE*)

Copyright © 2014 TJ Michaels

All rights reserved.

ALL RIGHTS RESERVED.

Formatted by IRONHORSE Formatting

ISBN-13: 978-0-9857874-6-2

PRAISE FOR THE NOVELS OF TJ MICHAELS

Silk Road

"An action packed thriller too hot to miss!" ~Lisa Renee Jones, national bestselling author

"Silk Road twisted and turned flawlessly. The characters were nothing short of fantastic." ~Booked and Loaded Reviews

"SILK ROAD is an entertaining urban fantasy romance that promises to captivate readers as good, evil, and something in between converge in a real page turner from beginning to end." ~R. Barri Flowers, bestselling Harlequin author of MURDER IN HONOLULU and MURDER IN MAUI

The Vampire Council of Ethics Series

"Interesting new world. Hot stuff!" ~Shayla Black, New York Times bestselling author

"CARINIAN'S SEEKER was a highly erotic, thrilling suspenseful, paranormal read that will blow your mind." ~Fallen Angel Reviews

"It had me rooting for their happy-ever-after as much as cheering their kick-ass assignments" ~Just Erotic Romance Reviews

"T.J. MICHAELS has done an astounding job of crafting a steamy hot suspenseful romance—" ~Romance Junkies

Spirit Bound Novels

"All in all, [On the Prowl] is a fun and delightful story with spicy sex and great suspense both in the love story and the plot." ~Just Erotic Romance Reviews

"Using heat, danger and tension, Egyptian Voyage will keep you glued to that edge of your seat as you go along for the ride. TJ Michaels has written a story that will fascinate, horrify and ultimately delight the reader." ~SensualReads.com

Forever December
"[Forever December] is a highly erotic, touching and sexy novella that will have you reaching for a tall, cold glass of water and a fan." ~Romance Divas

"Explosive love scenes will curl your toes and leave you fanning. Readers who love a flare for the dramatic with paranormal elements will certainly become fans of TJ Michaels." ~Romance Junkies

Jaguar's Rule
"The plot is flawlessly executed and the characters remain true." ~The Romance Studio

"T.J. MICHAELS knows how to write plot and passion in a most memorable way!" ~Fallen Angels Reviews

DEDICATION

To my family by blood, sisters from another mister, and brothers from another mother. Tam, Mike, Mindy and CVD, you guys have no idea how much your love and support meant to me while penning this book. Thinking back on all the conversations that led up to the idea for this series, both funny and not-so-funny, be assured there's a little bit of all of you in this novel! Strap in, it's time for takeoff!

To Softrock, Burton and Mizz Lovitt, you are fantastic for simply being wonderful friends for so many years. Your unwavering kindness and willingness to see your friends through thick and thin is immeasurable.

To EdenB and Wynde for being my MacKenzie's. Thank you so much for exercising great patience while I asked you a bazillion questions (((SMILE))). Oh, and Wyn, you rock for volunteering your husband to paint my motorcycle *wink*!

To Mr. Austin, without you this book would not have been possible. At all.

And to my readers, especially the ones who catch me on social networking sites—you are all so supportive, funny and lively. This writing thing wouldn't be nearly as much of a blast without you. I am so grateful.

CHAPTER ONE

Solie Shaw had been so deep in thought that the playful 'ding-da-ding-dong' of her phone startled her. She looked around her desk. It was covered with sticky notes of so many colors it was a fair representation of the rainbow. But where was her phone?

"Ah, there it is." It was partially hidden under the newest project plan she'd printed out. Her current tasks outnumbered her brain cells for sure. She had so much to do that there was no way she'd make all the deadlines. But she was totally grateful for the distraction of work given the recent drama that had engulfed her life.

Yes, she'd been tossed upside down by Hurricane Marcais—a wickedly handsome man who'd crashed into her world, burned it down around her, then rained so much *crazy* into the charred remains, she'd been totally swept out to sea and left to drown. The bastard.

Oh, yeah. Phone. She dug it from under the pile of papers and stared at the screen. Her head tilted a hard right as her gut did a freefall.

The caller id read *Marcais Dupree*.

"Damn. Speak of the devil."

The phone continued to play the special tune associated with his contact. All she could do was stare at the danged screen while commanding her stomach to stop running around underneath her skin.

Solie had learned from a friend that her now ex-dude had been trying to hook up with her, behind Solie's back. She'd been the third woman in a three-week span. So after calling him several times, Solie had left a very polite, though tear-filled voice message; ending what was left of their crumbling relationship. Part of her had hoped he would deny the other woman's claims. Again. Yet another part of her was glad to be done with it.

Marcais hadn't answered her very nice "fuck off" message, nor had he bothered to reply to the e-mail she'd sent a week later, wishing him well. She'd even included a special prayer written just for him. Even though she'd been nothing but an expendable replacement for his ex-wife, Solie had experienced a strange mix of pain and relief when he hadn't bothered to respond.

But all of that was weeks ago. It felt like an eon considering they'd lived together and seen each other every day for a year. He'd even talked of taking her with him overseas once he'd learned that the Army was reassigning him.

Finally the ringing stopped.

She took a deep breath and leaned over to scratch her shepherd, Mims, behind the ears. In that moment, Solie accepted a few things as fact.

First, if just seeing the man's name on the caller id could make her want to run and hide in a lockable closet, then she wasn't quite over the hell he'd brought into her life. A line from the famous movie, Tombstone, came to mind. Solie could even picture the snarl on Kurt Russell's face as he played a rather convincing Wyatt Earp. He'd promised a reckoning to a bad guy as he'd

2

bellowed, "And hell's coming with me! You hear?!" Well, Marcais Dupree had been an expert at ushering in emotional infernos.

Second, sheer determination to process the hurt in a healthy manner burst forward and brought her 'mad' along with it. She refused to be defeated, emotionally or otherwise. A few seconds later her phone dinged again—a text message. From *him*. And the damn phone wouldn't let her delete it without opening it first.

She clicked on the message and braced herself.

"Say what?" she asked to her empty office. Solie looked up to the ceiling wondering if she'd just read what she thought she had. Looking at the phone again had her shaking her head. Nope, the message hadn't morphed into something that actually made sense. It simply read, "Thank you for your e-mail. Hope to talk to you soon."

Really? Why now? What did he *really* want from her?

Instead of replying to the text message, Solie decided to do a little investigating. Maybe he'd decided to behave after all? She had no interest whatsoever in getting back together with Marcais, but a part of her still hoped that he'd meant at least one word of all of those declarations of love and care.

"So he couldn't respond to me telling him that I didn't want to see him again because a third woman told me he was chasing her; but he responds to an e-mail with a prayer in it? And a week or two *after* I sent it? Go figure." The words were half-snarled-half-mumbled to herself as her fingertips flew over the keyboard.

She logged into her private Kinkfest profile and skipped over to his page. Perhaps there was something there that would give her a clue as to why he was contacting her now.

There. There it was. His profile.

Solie's hand flew to her mouth on a gasp.

"Oh. My. God. Why do I always have to look? Why?"

Good question, because now she couldn't *unsee* it either. It was the greatest mind fuck of all and she'd walked right into it. She felt like one of the hobbits from the Lord of the Rings. Yep, she was a nosy chick from The Shire who'd looked at something she had no business. Now she was getting smacked by a damn orc for being nosey.

"Son of a bitch," she breathed. Her chest was heavy, as if someone had hit her in the middle of the sternum with Thor's hammer. Her heart beat a mile a minute and adrenaline pumped furiously.

"Fight or flight, Solie. Fight or flight?"

Three times she started to respond to what she saw posted on *his* wall for the world to see. And three times she stopped herself. Instead, she read it again…and again.

"I want to feel everything. I want to see you squirm in anticipation of what I will do to you. I want tease you with my fingers and feel you get wet. I want to feel you grip me as I push in and pull out. I want to see your pretty pussy hold me. When I pull out it looks like it wants to come with me. I want to wrap you in the rope that I bought just for you, to restrict your movements and leave my hands free to massage and tease other parts of your body.

I want to push deep, then deeper so I can watch your eyes widen because no one has ever been to that spot before. I want you to wear the fuck-me pumps I gave you because I can grab the heels and manipulate your legs to open you up. I love to watch your eyes roll back in your head, to hear you take that deep gasp of air as you reach and stretch for things that are not there.

I want you to beg me to fuck you, want to hear the

4

words because you say it just the way I like. I want to flip you over and take you from behind as I spank your perfect ass so I can see the slight redness of my hand print on your skin. I like that I can manhandle you and yet kiss you softly. I want to manipulate you anywhere at any time. I want to hear you scream as your toes curl when you come. I want to gently wipe your tears when you begin to cry from orgasm after orgasm.

And I can do all these things because you trust that I will never hurt you and that I have your best interests at heart. There is only you. I have no need of other toys. We are fluid-bonded and I wear you when we are done just as you wear me. Your scent is on me and mine is entwined with yours. Yes, I wear you. And you drip of me. I want to hold you afterward as you drift in a space that you have only found with me. I want to kiss you on your forehead, wrap my arms around you as I feed you chocolate while we lay on top of the sweat-soaked sheets. Because you are my submissive. And I love you."

She sat there for long moments with her hand over her mouth, eyes wide with disbelief. When emotions were finally a smidge under control, she slammed the laptop closed, stormed out of her office and down the hall. The leash was snatched off the hook near the front door as she headed to the truck with her dog on her heels.

The half-mile to the trails were a forgotten blur as she pulled into the parking area. The sky was as cloudy as her mood as she slipped the leash around her shepherd's thick neck and took off down the nearest path.

Then Solie did what she should have done the moment Marcais' text message had arrived—she hit the speed dial and called one of her very best friends.

Burton picked up on the second ring.

Oh thank God!

"Burton!"

5

"Solie? You okay?"

"Hell no I'm not okay! Oh my God, I just can't believe he did that. It's just so low and—"

"Whoa, whoa, whoa, what the hell happened?"

"I'm such an idiot, Burt. I just…I just can't believe I did it."

"Woman, what did you do?"

While Burton and Solie had never had a Dominant/submissive relationship—sexual or otherwise—there'd always been an undercurrent of tension in his presence that made her belly feel as if someone tugged on her insides. She still considered both him and Mac as her private play partners though they seldom ever played. Burton always took care of her…including punishing her if she needed it.

"He sent me a text message."

"He? You mean *that guy*? Solie tell me you didn't call him."

"I didn't, I swear. What I did was worse."

"Huh?"

"Instead of answering his call or responding to his text, I went and perved his Kinkfest profile. And he'd written a poem-like thing. Only it wasn't a poem. It was a story. About me."

"What?"

"You heard me. He started it off by saying, 'I want to…' but then everything after that was a recital of what happened between us in the bedroom."

"Are you shitting me?"

"No! I wish I was." Her eyes stung with tears, but she'd never get through the story if she started to cry now. After what Marcais had written she had every right to bawl her brains out, but that would have to come later. Right now, she had a confession to make. Solie picked up the pace, though she was practically running already.

"Look, Burt, he wrote a journal entry as if it was

something that he wanted to happen between him and someone else. He didn't use my name of course—"

"Of course."

"But the facial expressions that he says he wants to see during this act of supposed love were *my* facial expressions. *My* body language. *My* words. He practically described the way I orgasm, the cheap bastard."

"Oh man. That sounds brutal."

"Yeah, but that's not the worst part. He put at the end of it that this person should know that he has her best interest at heart because, and I quote, 'You are my submissive and I love you'."

Burt's low whistle filled the line. Yeah. She knew exactly what he was thinking.

"And the women he's been collecting like fucking baseball cards had filled his profile with all kinds of sappy shit. They were all like, 'oh, that's so sweet,' and 'oh I wish it were me' and 'oh she's so lucky' and all of this royal bullshit. I stood in my office and screamed."

"You mean kind of like you're screaming now?" Burton asked. And he was right. She was screaming at the top of her lungs. Hadn't even flinched when a terrified flock of birds burst into flight as she'd stormed past the tree they were roosting in. Must have scared them with her banshee impersonation. Even her dog looked at her as if she'd left her brains back at home in her office.

So much for control.

"Sorry," she mumbled.

"No worries. You have every right to yell to the rafters. He's basically taken something that was special and intimate between you two and turned it into bait for some other woman."

That pretty much summed it up.

"I wanted to call him up and tell him off. I wanted to

7

send him a private message or reply to his text in all caps telling him what a mind-fuck it was, the bastard. I wanted to scream, 'Hey asshole, I did that. I gave that. I fucking earned that! But you never loved me. You just came home to me late at night while you spent your afternoons and evenings sticking your dick into anything with a hole!"

She really was losing it now, but she just couldn't help it. A guy riding past her on a bike must surely think she was crazy. Solie didn't give a rat's rear end. Not at all.

"Well you know you shouldn't have looked, right Solie?"

Aw man. Burt had turned on his Dom-ly voice, which meant she was actually in trouble. And if she'd been thinking clearly she would have seen this coming. Must be Solie-The-Idiot Day or something. First, she'd walked right into a mind fuck of epic proportions with her ex-dude, and now she'd told all her business to one of the few people that could actually make her sorry— one her best friends and protectors, Burton Khrys.

"Solie?"

"Yes, I know I shouldn't have looked but—"

"There's a *'but'* in there somewhere? Really, woman?"

She kept her mouth shut. Smartest thing she'd done all day.

"You're well aware that this man is a textbook sociopath, yes?"

Sigh.

"Solie, I asked you a question." The words were spoken quietly, but there was no way in hell she missed the steel behind them.

"Yes, I'm aware he's a sociopath," she grumbled.

"And I've shared my experiences with you about people who have this disorder, which lines up with your own research. It's to be expected for a sociopath to pull some kind of shenanigan or another, right?"

She should write a song called, "Yet another sigh." Bleh. Instead, she growled out a plain old, "Yes."

"I'm not even going to ask you what you were thinking, Solie, but I will say that I'm sure you know better."

Oh here we go.

"Are you still going to the vendor fair at the C.S.P. tomorrow?" he asked.

That was a no brainer. The vendor fair at the Community for Sex Positivity was a twice a year event that she and her other best friend, MacKenzie, didn't miss. Many of the vendors were different each time, so there was always something cool and unique to be had.

"Yep, I'm going to the fair. Mac promised my niece that we'd get some new toys for her play bag."

"Okay. So, when I see you tomorrow I'm going to spank your ass for doing what you know you shouldn't have, which was perv *that guy's* profile. Agreed?"

Damn. She could simply say no. Burton wouldn't do anything without her consent. But she was in the wrong. There were no two ways about it. Not only had she connected the sociopathic dots when her relationship with Marcais began to head south, but Burt had confirmed her suspicion because he'd had plenty of experience with people like her former dude.

To make matters worse, Solie had reached out to Marcais' ex-wife to learn exactly what she was dealing with. That woman, who'd turned out to be a fabulous person, had also told her to expect the man to do something to re-establish communication with her. And if he couldn't do that, he would pull a mind fuck.

So yep, Solie had known the moment she'd read his message that Marcais wouldn't have reached out to her for the hell of it. He had a purpose, always. For someone like him it wasn't about love. It was about winning. About control.

In the end, Solie had royally worked herself into a tizzy behind something that could have been avoided. All she'd had to do was exercise a little restraint and stop long enough to think about what she was doing. Basically, she could have simply ignored *he who should not be named*. But nooo-ho-ho-ho. She just had to go and be nosy. Just *had* to see what Marcais was pitching when she knew she shouldn't.

And now, she'd tattled on herself to Burton? Forehead, meet desk. Yeah. That.

"Solie? I asked if you agree to the punishment."

Ugh. Burt knew she was so *not* an exhibitionist, regardless of her love of kink. So public spanking equaled absolute punishment in her book. Hell, she totally had this coming.

"Yes. I agree."

"And I'll spank your ass every time you perv his Kinkfest profile. Agreed?"

"Fine," she snarled into the phone.

"In fact, I'm driving down to Seattle just for you, darlin."

"Yay. I feel so special." The words were dead pan. Burton's responding laughter lifted her mood a bit.

Then he said, "But you are special, Solie. Just because a pathological liar and a serial cheater didn't treat you right, doesn't mean you deserved it. Woman, you should be treated like the amazing catch that you are. You're a queen bee and you know it."

She smiled a bit brighter. But still...

"Well I don't feel like a damn queen. I feel like an idiot. An idiot for not seeing the red flags earlier. For not cutting him off earlier. For not totally ignoring him. Look where it got me."

"Solie, don't be ridiculous. Sociopaths and narcissists

aren't stupid. They're very smooth, charming and look like the perfect guy or gal. Why? Because they are experts at manipulation. Didn't his ex say he cheated on her for almost eight years? And didn't she compliment you for cutting him off after barely one year? Can you imagine how hard it was for her to admit that?"

Still, it didn't make her feel any better. Her ego was beyond bruised. And now she was going to have a tender ass on top of that.

Just great.

* * * * *

With her phone plastered to her head yet again, Solie peered out the window of her office. The soft summer breeze had blown out the earlier clouds to reveal a clear blue sky. It reflected off of the waters of the Puget Sound and reminded her of her favorite piece of sparkling, deep-blue, topaz jewelry.

She twirled lazily in her office chair. Joy was instantaneous when the number she'd dialed was answered on the third ring, and a voice that brought to mind her favorite jazz singer greeted her with an upbeat "hello".

"Hey Mac! I totally agreed to let Burton spank me. Publicly."

"What? You agreed to let that Sasquatch put his hands on you? On your bare ass? Girl, you're a brave one." MacKenzie Ivers burst into a deep laugh that had the sides of Solie's mouth pulling up into a smile. Mac was a female version of Burton—best friends until one of them kicked and left the world for good.

"Girlfriend, you know he's not going to hold back. And his line of work makes him awfully strong."

Solie just sat and shook her head at herself as Mac reminded her that because Burton built houses and supervised work crews, he was a very strong man. Sometimes he had to do the suit and tie bit; when he met with his architects and clients. Other days it was ripped jeans, hard hats, work boots and lots of fantastically defined muscle.

Mac had introduced her to kink and protected her fiercely to this day. Many people thought BDSM was all about sex. For Solie, it was all about trust.

As such, Solie had explored the lifestyle for a few years before ever playing with anyone. Instead of wading into the deep without knowing how to float, she'd taken the time to learn what she liked and didn't like; as well as accept the advice and guidance of her friends. This lifestyle was like anything else—with the good and the bad; ups and downs; sane people and nutballs.

She'd also discovered that although she was a bad ass in the boardroom, she didn't prefer to be one at home. Solie owned a business and had a knack for running things. On the flip side, there existed a submissive side that was greatly satisfied by serving and giving to others. The result was Solie's most cherished nickname given to her by MacKenzie—the "fantabulous alpha bitch submissive of the universe".

When she'd finally been ready to actually jump into physical play, Mac, her very best girlfriend, had been the first to give her a flogger tasting. It had been the most fabulous birthday present ever. For days, Solie had preened in front of her mirror and grinned over the pretty marks left on her skin.

But right now her brow pulled down into a frown at the rest of the memory—that night at the Twilight Teahouse had been Solie's first time playing in public. Ever. And Marcais hadn't been there. He'd forgotten her birthday completely and then claimed he'd thought it was a day later.

But he hadn't shown up the next day.

Or the day after that.

Turned out that one of his other women had a birthday the day after Solie's, and he'd spent the weekend with that chick instead. So sure, he'd forgotten Solie's birthday because his mind had been elsewhere. Literally.

Mac and Burton had seen her through the good and the bad, which included the long list of Marcais' betrayals. They'd held their tongues each time Solie forgave the man, and gave advice only when asked for it. Her buds had listened to all the rants, and dried all the tears.

"Stop thinking about him, Solie." Mac's tone snapped her out of her musings. "I can tell by your silence after my sasquatch crack that you're thinking about *that guy*."

Mac wouldn't even speak Marcais' name, as if it would taint her soul or something. Actually, Mac described him as the shit on the heel of the antichrist, so maybe she did think his asshole-ish-ness was contagious.

"I can't help it, Mac. You know the human psyche doesn't work that way. I can't just turn it off as if it never happened. Besides, it's only been a few weeks since we broke up for good."

"Yes, I know. I just hate that you're in pain and there is nothing I can do about it. I know you have to process it, feel it. But damn it, Solie, I just fucking hate it."

A few moments of silence passed.

"Mac, I appreciate it. You know I love you, right girl?"

"And I love you right back. Damn it, I've gotta go, Sols. My two-thirty appointment is here."

"No worries. Go ahead and work your magic, oh architect extraordinaire," Solie said. The woman indeed one of the premier and sought-after architects in the Pacific Northwest. "One day I'm going to hire you to design my dream house."

"Hire me? Do you want to add a second spanking to your punishment, you crazy woman? You won't ever hire me. Whatever you need or want is yours. You know that. Now I'm going to ask you to do something that my therapist once suggested to me as I was going through my divorce."

Mac and her husband, Landon, had hit what seemed like an endless rough patch in their ten year marriage. Mac had wanted counseling but Landon voiced loudly and often that he didn't need any help because it was all Mac's fault—it didn't matter what *it* was. Mac had lifted her head, refused to be stomped on, and filed for a divorce that she'd bounced back from like a champ. In fact she'd processed that madness so completely that her husband, Landon, couldn't help but notice. He followed Mac's example, came to his senses and sought some good therapy. In the end, he'd come crawling back to Mac on hands and knees. Literally. Now, to everyone's grand relief, they were the happiest couple Solie knew.

"I want you to write down how you feel, Sols. No holds barred, no editing or altering. Just write it down. All of it. You're heartbroken and I understand better than anyone. You know that." Yes, she did know. Not too long ago, Mac had been through her own journey through the Seventh level's East Side of Hell. "And I know I told you to stop thinking about him, but that was a knee-jerk reaction. I'm sorry for that. Forgive me?"

"Of course, woman. So, what do you want me to do? Just write about my feelings?"

"Yes, but rather than dwell on all the ways this guy screwed you, concentrate on what you actually feel. So no 'he did this or that'. Instead make it, 'I, Solie, feel…', then fill in the blanks. Make sense?"

"Yep."

"And you don't have to share it, Solie. You're allowed to keep your own counsel and play this as close to the vest as you want. This is your thing. Yours. You own it; do it the way you see fit as long as you stay on this side of functional. No dysfunctional bullshit. Agreed?"

"Agreed."

"Okay, I gotta run. Catch you later?"

"I know we're going to the fair together, but will you stick around for...you know?"

"Do you honestly think I'd miss the chance to watch Burton paddle your ass?"

"No paddle. Just bare hand."

"Not the point. The question was, do you think I'd miss that? Hell no!" Mac laughed, full and honestly. "Wouldn't miss it for the world because you know your goofy ass deserves it."

Did her friends have to be right all the damn time? Solie shook her head at herself, said her goodbyes and turned her attention back to work. And every time her brain tried to skip off to "dwell-on-Marcais-land" Solie deliberately squashed those thoughts. Instead, she concentrated on the anomalies between the databases in front of her. Reverse engineering someone else's work was a pain in the ass, but it was necessary if she was going to figure out why the script she'd written to move data from one system to another wasn't working.

Normally it would be annoying as hell to find such huge differences between systems, but right now it was a hell of a welcome distraction. When eyeballs began to cross and hands trembled a bit, Solie looked down at her now-buzzing phone. Earlier during a brief moment of common sense—she seemed to be sorely lacking in that particular area lately—she'd set her alarm for seven o'clock this evening to keep herself from over doing it on her day.

She hadn't actually eaten since she'd gotten back from walking the dog and screaming at Burton at lunchtime. No wonder her stomach felt like an empty, wind-swept cavern.

"Well, at least I remembered to drink water," she grumbled at herself.

Thankfully, Mac knew her so well she'd swung by a couple of hours ago on her way to Twilight Teahouse. The woman had run in, waved as she passed Solie's office, said something about plugging in a crockpot and then run out again.

Solie had peeked out of her window and caught a glimpse of Mac's outfit as she jumped back into her car—black knee high boots with buckles up the side, a burgundy leather corset with matching bolero jacket over a sleek black cat suit. My goodness, it was a combination of Selene the Underworld Death-dealer and a sexy, flogger-toting Hollywood starlet. Mac had pulled out of the driveway and was gone as quickly as she'd arrived.

After a quick pit-stop to the bathroom for a wash-up, Solie found that crockpot on her kitchen counter and happily dished up a big bowl of steak chili. This time, when she returned to her office, it was for some self-healing rather than work.

She'd suppressed her thoughts all day. Now she followed Mac's advice and wrote it down. She called her journal entry, Heartbreak and Monkey Balls.

* * * * *

Heartbreak and Monkey Balls

Heartbreak sucks hairy monkey balls and makes this girl wish that people came with warning labels, including myself. But you know what else heartbreak does?

It makes you want to crawl into your hole and never

come out again, though you know you have too much shit to do to hide yourself away.

Makes you scream, "Big girls don't cry!" while you blow through a box of tissues and a pint of Ben and Jerry's.

Makes you want to scream, "I hate you!" while your heart bleeds and cries, "I love you."

Makes you wonder what you did to deserve this, when you already know the answer is 'nothing'.

Makes you wonder why you aren't good enough. Even while others tell you how awesome you are, in your mind you're thinking, "Yeah, sure - I'm so awesome that I wasn't worth keeping or fighting for."

Makes you want to shank him in the face, yet have the gauze, cloth tape and peroxide ready to sooth him.

Makes you want to put up a "Fuck You and Your Mama!" sign, though you know you were put here to serve and upgrade your partner, family and community.

Makes you wonder why he would stray and end up with nothing, when you'd already given heart, home, money, love, body, mind...everything.

Makes you want to close the door, even while you know you must keep the door open to allow your blessings to come through.

Makes you feel like a used piece of tissue, tossed away for a new piece of temporary ass, even though you know you are spun silk, gold and frankincense. Priceless.

Makes you want to become the ultimate dysfunctional bitch persona with a closed heart, even when you know you're not capable of doing so.

Makes you want to hold and nurse a grudge...when in truth, you've already forgiven.

Makes you want to run for the hills while you long for second chances.

Makes you want to know why, yet makes you NEVER

want to know.

Makes you want to yell and scream...but you can't move past the hurt to get to the anger that would allow you to do so.

Makes you wish you were a crazy vindictive bitch, though you just don't have it in you.

Makes you want to punch people in the face who say, "Don't worry, you'll find someone better" when what you wanted...was him.

Makes you want him to admit that he doesn't care about you, even while you never *want him to* ever *admit such a thing.*

Makes your stomach tie in knots knowing he'll simply go on to the next one, while you still hope he truly finds happiness.

Makes you feel sorry for yourself because you are alone yet again, and sorry for him because there is no one else in the world like you...and he has lost you forever and has no idea why.

* * * * *

Yep, that summed it up pretty well.

And Mac had been right. When Solie pressed the save button, closed her journal and turned off her computer, she felt just a tad bit better.

CHAPTER TWO

Saturday rolled around much too quickly.

Mac swung by, picked Solie up and they headed into the city. As they rode, Mac chatted about this, that and the other. Solie appreciated that Mac just let her sit there quietly and ride along to the upbeat music she had pumping through her speakers. There was no need to point out her case of nerves. The fact that Solie was so quiet was a minor miracle in itself.

Mac had even pulled off the freeway and queued into a drive-through, yet Solie hadn't noticed until a hot cup was pressed into her hand followed by a half-dozen nom-noms in a warm open bag.

"Salted caramel Krispy Kreme's? Oooh, yummily. Woman, you are a goddess."

"Yes, I am," Mac said. "And I have ice in a cooler in the backseat in case your ass needs it after your Burton spanking," Mac joked. "Oh, and I have some paddled-butt-be-gone cream, too."

Solie laughed at that one, took another bite of delicious sugar-coma-in-a-bag and chased it down with piping hot coffee.

"No butt-be-gone for you?" Mac asked. "How about some anti-sasquatch-big-scary-paddle-hand spray?"

Solie choked on her coffee.

The levity helped, but she was still nervous. Was it because she'd be getting a public spanking or because Burton was the one giving it? She totally trusted the man. Had for years. He was ridiculously handsome and something about him had always drawn her although they'd never been intimate in more than a "bestie" kind of way.

Now, with the culmination of all the recent theatre in her life, she stopped to take inventory of her emotions. And with Burton, there was no doubt of a spark of…something. Often she thought on the sound of his voice as he spoke, his quiet but compelling manner. And the impact of his Caribbean Sea-colored gaze when all his attention was on her.

He was an alpha, through and through. Dominant. All the time. It was his nature. Not one of the dark and broody types, yet it still wasn't something he had to tell or declare to anyone. It was just who he was.

And now she had something else to consider— Burton's hands on her skin, caressing her flesh to deliver a mix of what she needed, wanted and feared.

At six-feet even, Burton was perfectly proportioned, a bit on the stocky side and *more* than a bit on the handsome side. In fact, the man was all kinds of pretty, in a Marine "hoorah" kind of way. Known for his skill with floggers, paddles, dragon tail whips and even Hojōjutsu rope technique, Burton Khrys was in demand. His ability to read the needs of his partner, whether they were male or female, was downright uncanny. He could have damn near any woman he wanted in their local kink community. In fact, he'd been constantly sought after since he'd removed his collar from his last submissive.

But Burt was picky. He believed in wholeheartedly

and thoroughly caring for those he considered his. He put a lot of time and energy into his relationships, whether they were of a sexual nature or not. As such, he was very selective about who he gave all that energy to. He didn't believe in casual anything. With Solie, Mac and very few others, Burton cared in action, not just word.

He really was the complete package.

Parked right across the street from the Community for Sex Positivity building, Solie took a deep breath and climbed out of Mac's car. Maybe she was twitchy because it was a punishment scene? Nah. It wasn't as if she'd never been in trouble before with her own Dominant. Well, former Dominant.

So, what was this gut-with-butterflies-in-flight thing going on here?

Passing the tables of vendors, a set of sterling silver claws caught her eye.

"Oooh, Mac, look at those. Tooty would love the ones with the red powder finish," Solie said quietly.

"Speaking of Tooty, where is your niece anyway? I'm surprised she isn't here to witness this ass paddling?"

"She wanted to be here. I still can't believe I told her about it considering she thinks I should have snagged Burton years ago. She can't believe we're still just friends."

As they stood admiring the wares on the table, a couple of guys she'd seen at Twilight Teahouse walked past. She couldn't remember their names, but they were always together and dressed in head-to-toe black leather with spikes and crap everywhere. She almost laughed when one of them looked at her, then whispered to the other, "Hey, isn't that the bossy control freak chick that makes Doms quake in their boots? I heard she was a scary bitch."

Mac pinned them with a glare. They glared right back but kept on moving.

Well, Solie could be a lot to handle. She readily admitted that. But those who knew her well understood where she was coming from. She was the chick who got shit done. The end. It was a valuable trait in a submissive who was born to be more than a damn doormat.

Mac picked up a paddle. The handle was beaten metal with leather wrapped around it. She handed it to Solie. This time, she did laugh at the words "feisty bitch" carved into the wood.

"This is awesome, Sols. Maybe the claws and this paddle? I know the people who operate that particular armory. All their stuff is handmade. They have their own forges and everything. Ever want a tour of the place, let me know. Oh! There's our guy."

Solie gazed toward the other end of the large banquet style space to where Mac was looking. Burton stood there, leaning casually with one shoulder against a wall watching her. The moment their eyes met, he began moving toward them. Breath stuck in her throat at the huge, genuinely brilliant smile he sported as he took her in. It totally undid her.

"Nice outfit."

She looked down her body at the tasteful, but short, little red dress she'd sported today. The top was hand embroidered with swirls and little flowers done in a darker hue than the dress itself. Mid-thigh, the cut was tasteful yet sassy. Matching red strappy sandals completed the ensemble.

"Thank you." She gave him a hug, as was their habit. The moment he'd touched her, the jangling nerves quieted. Huh. She'd have to give that some thought…after. The typical warmth and safety of being in Burt's arms remained even after he'd gone on to hug

Mac.

"See anything interesting today?" he asked. "How's your bag full before you've even seen the whole place?" he asked, then took a swig from a tall paper cup. The faint scent of coffee and caramel declared his favorite poison—caramel macchiato with double whipped cream.

"I saw a cool set of surgical steel fingertip claws for my niece—"

"Yeah, and that's probably the only thing she didn't buy yet," Mac teased.

"Oh hush. Anyway, I got a unique pair of cuffs, too. I've never seen leather cuffs in that particular shade before. And they were so pretty next to some red bamboo rope I'm determined to try out."

"Rope? You want to be a rigger?" Burt asked.

"Nah, but I wouldn't mind being a rope bunny. I figure if I have my own rope it'll be good energy to attract someone who isn't crazy but is good with rope just the same."

"Hmm." And that was all Burton said. If his eyes were any indication, he wasn't all that excited about the idea. Interesting.

The three of them made their way past a number of booths, chatting as they went. At this moment, this seemed like any other time they'd hung out together—the three of them making small talk, cracking jokes and making plans for the following weekend.

Finally they made it into the building's main play room; which was large and open, with lots of stations throughout. There were winches for rope suspension, tables for everything from massage to fire cupping. For the edge players, there were spots for impact play, padded X's called Saint Andrews Crosses, as well as a crap-ton of spanking benches, which reminded Solie of little padded picnic tables. For a moment, she imagined a polka dot table cloth spread over one of them with her laid out on top as she waited to be served as a main course…to Burton.

Shaking her head to clear it of the unsettling thought, Solie looked around, just as she did every time she came to this particular event.

The place was nothing like the Twilight Teahouse, but it wasn't expected to be. The C.S.P. was one of the Seattle area's best known kinky spots. It was located, of all places, partially under an old freeway. The space was comfy in a 'worn old pair of slippers' kind of way, while the Twilight was more like kitten heels.

"Are you ready, Solie?" Burt asked.

What the hell kind of question was that? Of course she wasn't ready. This man, her very best friend and confidante, had big, thuddy, paddle hands. A woman would have to be nuts if she weren't at least a little apprehensive about having those hands on her bare ass.

She'd watched him play at the local dungeons and the man was an expert at giving a spanking, for both punishment and pleasure. Was she afraid he'd hurt her? Not in the least—she totally trusted Burt. But she also knew that she'd been in the wrong. So, no, she was nowhere near ready. But a deal was a deal.

With a huff and a sigh, she said, "Okay, let's do this."

And in a flash, Burt moved.

"Get up on the fucking bench, Solie."

Solie straddled the spanking bench and allowed Burt to push and pull her into the position he wanted her using her hair as a modern day steering wheel. In this moment he was the epitome of a gentleman who wasn't a gentle man.

"Now, you know why you're getting a spanking don't you, Solie?"

The words were a forceful growl against her ear, spoken just loud enough for her to hear, but not anyone in the now-gathering crowd. This is what she got for agreeing to get a spanking at the local vendor fair. Nothing like a bit of public humiliation. Bleh.

"Yes. I looked when I shouldn't have."

"Do you agree that he's playing you? Be honest, as always."

"Yes."

"And?"

"And I walked right into it."

"Are you going to do it again?"

"No."

"Why not?"

"Because he doesn't deserve my attention and I don't want my ass set on fire again."

"Good girl. Here we go." He eased her dress up just past her hips so her butt was exposed, but the front of her thighs were covered. Burt burst out laughing once he got a good look at the bulls-eye pattern on her barely-there underwear.

"Wait. Can I have a safe word after you're done laughing?"

"No. This is a punishment. There is no safe word, no warm up and no negotiation. Understand."

Yes, she did. When she'd been particularly bratty with *he who shall not be named,* she'd consented to the same rules. But she was grateful that Burton has asked anyway because in this particular game, one never assumed. Safety was always first.

This was new territory for their friendship. Burton had offered to become her protector the moment he learned how Marcais had been trolling around. But in all the years she'd known him, they'd only ever done some light play together, and never anything sexual.

"Do you consent, Solie?"

"Yes."

"Good. Four on each cheek, okay?"

She nodded and the second her head stopped moving

the first blow landed. Solie grunted under the impact. Holy shit, the man spanked hard. And then the second smack landed. Then the third and fourth.

He stopped, leaned down and asked her. "All right?"

She nodded.

Skin warmed quickly as the blood underneath rushed to the areas of impact. On the other cheek, the next smack landed, and with it came a particular sting that reminded her of a flogger more than a bare hand.

When Burton was done, he spoke quietly into her ear again.

"Do you need another one?"

Yes she did. Really, really needed this. Needed the impact to release the tears that welled up in her chest. But they weren't tears of physical pain. They were tears of anguish from the emotional shredding she'd endured at Marcais' hands, both in and after their relationship. Tears of healing. Even tears of joy that it was over and she'd survived.

"Yes, please," she whispered.

After a few more smacks, Burton gently pulled down her dress and helped her up off the spanking bench.

"You did good, Sol," Mac said.

She threw her arms around Burt's waist, buried her head against his chest and sobbed her heart out.

"That's it," Burt said. "Let it out. Release it. Holding it inside isn't good for you."

After a few moments, he asked, "So, tell me why you're crying."

Her words were muffled against the damp fabric of his shirt. "I feel like such an idiot. I can't believe I was so stupid. I fell for a charmer who could give two shits about me, and then I go and look to see what he's up to and he's busy writing about me to impress someone else. Several someone else's. And he didn't love me, Burt!" She sobbed. "He said that the person in the writing was his sub and he loved her. But he didn't love me. Before he moved out he said he loved me, but he didn't." She knew she was practically screeching but now that the dam had burst, she couldn't plug it up again.

"He didn't love me, Burt. He didn't. He didn't! God, he was so mean to me. He yelled and screamed at me when all I did was give and give and give. He treated me like shit. And he cheated with the very types of women he swore he didn't want. Were they so much better than me? Did they have something that I didn't? Why? Why would he do that to me?"

And she cried until she was exhausted and in need a German chocolate cake. And perhaps a new pair of shoes.

And after she got herself together, Solie's two best friends took her to go get both.

* * * * *

Solie took the leash off her shepherd and the both of them hopped back into the SUV and were home in less than five minutes. "This is becoming a habit, Burton. Don't get me wrong, I'm enjoying the summer sun and trail walking, but the circumstances suck ass."

"Well, I'm not happy that you're still in contact with him, Solie."

She stomped to a halt just inside her front door. Wait. Had she left it unlocked? Must have. Whatever. She was too pissed to care right now.

"No. Just no. I am not going to let you accuse me of something I did not do. I am *not* in communication with him, damn it. I reached out to this latest chick in hopes that she'd seen some of my jewelry. Actually, it's my niece Tooty's jewelry. It's all Native American beadwork. Handmade stuff that can't be replaced. We've been collecting it for twenty years."

"Why do you think he took it?"

"Other than the fact that it was in the same garage as his stuff, and it disappeared when he moved out? Or maybe the fact that he's a pathological liar and a thief? He thinks I don't know that he once gave his ex-wife some jewelry that belonged to someone else. Or that I don't know that the motorcycle jacket he gave me, you know, the one that he tried to take with him when he moved out, actually belonged to his ex-wife. It's her fucking coat. And he gave it to me as if he'd bought it for me. There's so much he thinks I don't know. In fact, I know enough to write a fucking horror novel. He'd have a mutated cow if he knew that because of his foolishness, his ex-wife and I—"

"What's her name again?"

"His ex-wife? Her name's Whitney. And she and I have become fast friends. In fact, she's as cool as I don't know what."

"Okay, then who's this latest girl on Kinkfest?" Burt asked.

"Her name is Karen. I sent her a note because she was a friend of a friend of a friend. I swear I didn't know she was literally fucking Marcais. After I found out, I sent her another note telling her that I was his ex because I didn't want her to feel as if I'd been trying to play her."

"That's fair. Thoughtful, actually," Burt said.

"Well I agree, or I did agree until she told me that she thought I looked familiar. She'd seen pictures of me on Marcais' Facebook page."

"Excuse me?"

"Yeah, that's what I thought. Whitney told me that he was probably still on Facebook doing dirty, but was hiding it from me, but I didn't want to believe it in spite of all the other crap I knew he'd done. Marcais swore from the moment we got together that Facebook was off limits for him. So why would he let this Karen chick be friends with him there, but hide it from me?"

"Let me guess, because he had a bunch of other chicks on there, too, right?"

"Right." More than right. In fact, Karen had told her that she'd been seeing Marcais for quite a while and how wonderful he was and how sad she was about the fact that the military was sending him overseas and how she'd miss him and blah, blah, blah.

"Damn it, Burt, I swear it seems every time I think I'm progressing, healing and moving on, I get some new piece of information that keeps this man as front and center in my life. He's like a wet booger…just stuck on me and I can't wipe him off! Why can't it be over already?"

To hear Karen talk of how they'd fallen so deeply for each other while he'd been living in Solie's house had cut her anew. Never mind the fact that they were supposed to be a monogamous couple. It made the acid churn in her stomach to know that a woman Marcais was cheating with had fallen in love with his monkey ass. Just like Solie had fallen in love with him.

"You know what's going to happen, Sol. Marcais is going to drop this Karen girl like a hot rock as soon as he finds out the two of you had a conversation. Why? Because she was supposed to be a secret. The only one who didn't know it was her. If he doesn't dump her now, he'll dump her as soon as the next one is in place. That's the MO. It's what sociopaths do."

"Doesn't make me feel any better, Burton."

"Just remember that to a man, pussy is very different from love. She was just a lay."

Solie knew Burton was right and she almost felt sorry for Karen. Almost.

But her compassion for the other woman was damn near on empty because Karen admitted that she'd *known* Marcais was in a relationship with someone else…with

Solie. But she hadn't given a rat's ass. Instead, she'd spent time with Marcais anyway. Slept with him anyway. Got hooked on him anyway. Took pictures of her having sex with him anyway.

"Mac bring you lunch today, Sols?"

"Yep. It's homemade clam chowder." She spooned up a big bowl while talking to Burton. Now, sat down at her desk, took a bite and moaned in appreciation. Fog had rolled in and it had gone from sunny to chilly. The thick creamy soup, made hearty with a ton of seafood, potatoes, savory spices and herbs, warmed her tummy.

"Good to hear you're not skipping meals. It's a bad habit and it's something you do way too often."

"I'm working on it, Burt. Seriously."

"Work harder. I'd hate to have to dole out more punishment."

She giggled when he said, "Then again, you have such a perfect ass I may have to make up something to get you in trouble just to get my hands on you again."

Burton. Was. Flirting!

And she had no idea what to do with it, other than acknowledge the wiggle in her tummy that signaled an impending bout of giddiness.

Then she remembered what they'd been talking about.

"You know what, Burt? I wonder if Karen knows that Marcais posted pics of them on the internet having unprotected anal sex."

She closed her eyes and shook her head trying to dislodge the image—Marcais' thick cock disappearing into Karen's willing body. The woman had held herself open for him, little pools of sweat gathered at the base of her spine. Her own fingers dug into her flesh. One of her fake fingernails had been broken, while the others were coated with glittery-blue polish. Marcais' cock had been slick with her juices. And no condom.

It was forever branded into Solie's brain.

A brain she wished she could just pluck from her head, sit down somewhere else and let it cool off for a while. Because in addition to the hurt, Solie was mad as hell.

Her dude—correction, *former* dude—had had unprotected sex with another woman, taken a picture of it, and was stupid enough to post it online. And yes, the date on the photo was *before* Solie had broken it off for good.

"It doesn't matter, Sols. As soon as he finds out that Karen spoke to you, she's history."

The next day, Burton was proven right.

After her typical early-morning wake-up ritual of showering, throwing on whatever she felt like, then practically dunking her head in a pot of coffee, Solie walked into her office. Karen's note was the first one in her email inbox. The woman had sent her a message telling her that Marcais was angry because the two women had spoken with one another. He was livid that Karen had told Solie the truth. And after he'd told the woman off as if she were some two-bit crack whore, he'd blocked her on Kinkfest and all the other social media sites.

Poor thing. Solie almost felt bad.

Until her phone rang just before lunch.

It was her doctor.

Marcais was the gift that just kept on giving…which unfortunately included a sexually transmitted disease.

An angry and hurt Solie transformed into a nuclear-hot Solie. The doctor had to report her condition to the state and the state would report it to the Center for Disease Control. After firing off a note to inform Marcais that he'd infected her, Solie headed to the pharmacy. One hour and a massive dose of antibiotics later, Solie pondered an issue that had been tapping at her brain since the doctor had called earlier.

She knew that Marcais was *not* going to return her calls or her texts. How could she make sure he got tested and treated? There had to be a way to keep him from pretending that none of this was happening.

Mind made up she made a few calls to some friends who happened to be stationed at the same Army base as him. Shortly after, Solie was voice-to-voice with Marcais' First Sergeant. And she didn't hesitate to lay out all the dirt, down to the last detail.

Thankfully, the sergeant was willing to help Solie out. The man wasn't happy that one of his soldiers was smack dab in the middle of such foolishness, had passed her cooties and played her dirty. Not to mention that particular soldier was soon headed out of the country to get away with it all.

But not anymore. He was going to have to face the music now that his command was aware of what he'd been up to.

Yep. Karma was one saucy bitch…and today she was Solie's best friend.

Sitting in her office like a zombie, Solie stared at a blank computer screen with the events of the day playing over in her mind like a bad B-movie. She picked up the phone and called Mac, who was quickly angry on her behalf.

And though she felt a bit better after Mac threatened to slip a castration pill into Marcais' food somehow, it didn't make the tight knot in the middle of her chest go away.

She needed something, someone else.

An hour later her doorbell rang.

She opened the door and her mouth dropped wide open.

It was Burton, who promptly informed her that dinner was on its way before shooing her into the living room.

Mac came in right behind him with her arms full of said dinner. She pecked Solie on the cheek and disappeared into the kitchen

Solie's eyes were instantly filled with tears. "You guys are too much."

"We care about you, woman. Now sit." Burton pointed to the couch and gave her the I-dare-you-to-argue look.

Burton turned on a movie that they'd all seen a million times so they could talk if they wanted to. Fifteen minutes later, Mac shoved a plate into her hands. The last thing she wanted was food, but she didn't fuss. Besides, she just didn't have the bandwidth for a fight. At all.

With dinner done and some blow-'em-up action movie exploding in the background Solie broke down and the tears poured out of her.

Pulled into Burt's lap, Solie found herself wrapped in strong arms as he whispered his care and concern into her ear.

The anger melted away, leaving a pool of bubbling pain in its place. And for the second time in as many days, Solie bawled her eyes out and soaked the front of Burton's shirt.

God, she was so damn tired of crying over someone who wasn't worthy to sniff her farts. Someone who was currently pretending as if she'd never existed. Someone who was a total douche canoe.

This was it. The last time she would give the memory of Sir Hell the power to level her. As of now, she was done.

Would she hurt awhile longer? Probably so. Denial would get her nowhere. But would she allow all her thoughts and emotions to be focused on the searing pain of betrayal? Hell no.

So Solie let it out and cried until she had no tears left.

Cried until she was so worn out she fell asleep in Burt's lap. The last thing she remembered was hearing Mac say that Landon had come to pick her up. She'd sweetly pecked Solie on the cheek as Burton tucked her into bed.

And Solie passed into a world of dreams filled with darkness, lava and fire with *he who should not be named* at the receiving end of a red hot poker up the ass.

Ah, justice.

CHAPTER THREE

The bedroom was always chilly this early in the morning. Today, Solie didn't feel any of it. Soothing energy rolled off of the man next to her—a man who'd tucked her in last night and stayed with her to make sure she was okay.

And Burton's presence warmed her from the inside out while his solid body warmed her from the outside in.

Yep, best of both worlds.

Solie ducked her head under the covers, mashed her face into his chest and wrapped her arms around him.

She took a deep breath. Fabric softener from her blankets and the natural masculine scent of her best friend filled her until she was drunk-n-drowsy. This wasn't the first time one of her friends had slept over, however this particular buddy had never slept in her bed. Especially not with her in it.

As she snuggled closer, the first thought that came to her muzzy mind was…safety. Not in a physical sense, though surely Burt could take care of her in that way, but this was more of an inner peace. A "my head and heart are safe with this guy" kind of thing. It was a knowing that unfurled in her belly. Rang in her head. Filled her up.

And the second thought? Well, that was easy—*damn he's hawt!*

"Solie? Wake up, honey."

Solie stretched with a half-smile-half-frown. "No wanna wake up. Comfy."

Burton's arms loosened as if he were about to get up. It was obvious he didn't really want to when his hold tightened again.

And the thought that he wanted to stay exactly where he was made Solie feel all manner of gooey inside— something she'd never quite experienced with *that other guy*. She wondered why considering that she'd loved Marcais. Truly loved him. But there was a piece of herself that she hadn't truly given over. Perhaps she'd known all along that he was playing her while a part of her soul hoped she'd been wrong.

"This is interesting," Burt whispered against her hair before dropping a gentle kiss on the top of her bed-head. "We've been friends for years and now, I—"

Solie stiffened, unsure of whether to eagerly anticipate what he was going to say, or prepare to flee. Burt stopped mid-sentence, took in a deep unsteady breath and blew it out. Arms tightened more around her body, then he let go and got out of bed.

Solie sat up, pulled the cover to her chin and pulled her knees up to her chest. Suddenly she felt so…cute.

"Why the blush, Sols?"

She didn't answer. Instead she simply shrugged and kept her mouth shut. This *kawaii* thing wasn't something typical. After all, she was a bitch on wheels every day, all day long as she ran her company. Sexy? Sure. Kick ass? Yep. Cute? Not so much. But there was no disputing that Burton just seemed to bring it out of her.

Or maybe it was the Hello Kitty shorts-and-tank top pajamas she wore. A set given to her by the very man peering down at her from beside the bed.

God, something about Burt rang her bell. And right now, she didn't really care what it was or why. In spite of the emotional roller-coaster she'd been on, there was one truth she didn't bother to dispute—she trusted this man. Completely.

He'd been her friend through all her ridiculous bullshit even while in the midst of his own heartbreak. While Mac was going through her on-again-off-again divorce with her husband, Landon, Burt was there. He was the genuine article when it came to loyalty minus naiveté or games.

And here he stood in her bedroom looking all kinds of yummy in a pair of tented—whoa, wait, *tented!*—boxers and a fabulously formed bare chest sprinkled with fine black down that arrowed to a very, very happy trail.

Oh my God, definitely tented boxers.

Burton's hair was a mop of jet black waves, cut short on the sides and a little longer on top. She almost smiled at the way it stuck up all over his head, glossy and inviting to her fingertips. Eyes so clear and crystalline blue they brought to mind one of those deep pools at the top of a glacial mountain under a clear sky.

Had she noticed how gorgeous he was before? Sure. But she'd never allowed herself to dwell. He'd belonged to someone else…and so had she.

But now she looked her fill after having spent the night being consoled in his arms. And Burton Khrys was just…wow.

And did she mention the tented boxers? The package beneath the fabric seemed long, thick and inviting. And it was all for her? Then again, maybe he always had some serious morning wood and it had nothing to do with her at all?

"Stay there. I'll be right back," he said.

A certain something about Burton—a something she'd been able to ignore before—seemed so close to the skin that it was almost tangible. And when he left the room, it left with him. And just that quickly, she missed it. Him. Whatever.

Six minutes later—but who was counting right?—Burton walked back into the bedroom and brought the scent of toothpaste and that certain *whoosh* of masculine energy with him.

He motioned with his head and said, "Scoot."

She immediately moved over and he set a tray down in front of her. Burt snatched some tissues out of the box next to the bed, pressed them into her fingers, and then put his attention back on the tray.

Solie looked down at her hand and back up at Burton.

"You're going to need it, Sol."

She was going to need tissue? This couldn't possibly be good.

Before she could ask why, he picked up her favorite porcelain mug and a small glass of half and half off the breakfast tray. A splash of cream soon joined what smelled like Italian roast coffee.

He handed the hot mug to her and said, "No sugar for you. Do you need to test your blood sugar first?" Yep—a gentleman who, beneath the skin, was not a gentle man. And she loved the contrast. Always had.

Solie tried not to compare him to her former dude but it was impossible. Why? Because Marcais knew she was diabetic but had never once asked if she needed to check her blood sugar or anything else, for that matter. Instead, he'd bring her all manner of sugary crap as gifts, then get mad at her when she couldn't eat it.

Okay, squash that. Back to the present.

"No, I'm fine. My doctor told me that a lot of times

my fasting blood sugar doesn't really measure how well I'm doing. It's what happens after I eat that tells her whether my body is doing what it should or not."

While she made small talk, Burt was busy grabbing a little brown bottle off the nightstand, retrieved a single tablet and pressed it into her palm.

"Thank you," she said as she popped the medicine into her mouth and chased it down with a gulp of coffee bean heaven. She moaned as she swallowed and then peeked over the rim of her mug at her friend. As she sipped, Solie almost smiled into the brew at Burt's lopsided, but totally smug, grin.

He was racking up brownie points. And he knew it.

Cheeky bastard.

With the tray moved over to the dresser, Burton sat down right in front of her and looked her square in the eye. Her cup paused halfway to her mouth.

"Listen, Solie. I know when you look at me you see someone who's been active in the BDSM community for years, someone who enjoys impact play and being a basic mean old man…"

Old? He was one year older than her? She raised an inquisitive brow, but didn't interrupt.

"I also know that you know me better than anyone else. And I have a proposition for you, none the less."

A prop-a-what? Was he serious?

She braced herself. Hard. But not out of fear like with Marc…

No. Nope. Keep it here, Solie.

And she would remind herself a million times a day if that's what it took to move on toward healing.

"I know you're on the rebound. But if I can take your pain, any of it, Solie, I want to do that for you. You could use the release, the catharsis."

Well he was right on that particular point, but there was more to this than Burt's desire to help her relieve the big ball of emotional tension she'd been carrying around. So she sipped her coffee and waited for the other shoe to drop. And God, she hoped that particular shoe was her size—nine medium, thank you very much.

"I've always been honest with you, Sols. It's been a long time since we discussed any feelings for each other, and understandably so. We've both been in relationships with others for years. I'm grateful because it allowed us to be good friends with no physical baggage between us. Still, you know I've found you attractive in every way, for a very long time. My timing is shitty, I'm sure, but it's the truth."

No wonder he'd handed her the tissue a few moments ago. Damn eyes were starting to tear up without her permission.

"Please tell me those are tears of happiness."

She cocked her head in genuine surprise.

"I may be able to anticipate some of your needs, woman, but I'm nowhere near a mind reader. I have no idea what's running through your head, or whether I'm making you happy or sad right now."

So she smiled because that's all she could manage just now.

"Okay, happy then?"

She nodded.

"Good," he said with a relieved sigh. "Back to my little monologue…. Shit!" Then he jumped up and flew out the door.

"Well, wow," she grumbled to herself. The snarl turned into a grin when the smoke detector blared. In fact, Solie stifled a very unladylike snort. Neither of them had ever been good at cooking. Thankfully Mac and her husband, Landon, usually took care of that particular task whenever they had dinner and movie night at any of their homes.

Back in the bedroom, Burton presented her with a

small plate of perfectly crisp bacon and two of the most burnt English muffins she'd ever seen.

She laughed. Just couldn't help it. And thankfully, Burt had a good sense of humor and joined in.

"Uh, since this is still smoking I think I'll just leave the bacon and go toss the rest." He picked up the charred bread with a napkin and started to head out again. "Be right back. Windows are open in the kitchen."

Before he could get up, Solie's free hand shot out and took him by the wrist. The moment he stilled she snatched her hand back. She hadn't meant to snatch him like that, but there was no way he could leave the room. Not now.

His expression was wide open and she was glad to see that he wasn't offended that she'd grabbed him like he owed her money. Instead, he simply stood and waited for her to say whatever was on her mind.

"Wait, Burt. I-I really need to finish this conversation. Please."

Instead of leaving, burnt bits were tossed into the little waste basket next to the nightstand and he sat back down.

"What are you thinking about?" he asked.

"I want to know when your feelings for me moved past friendship."

"Beautiful, they've always been past friendship. But I was with someone else at the time, and so were you. I don't cheat, and I wouldn't disrespect you or the person I was dating at the time by asking you to be the 'other woman'. Having you as a friend wasn't my way of settling for what I couldn't have. It was important to me to be a good friend to you because you deserve it. And you've been a good friend to me right back. Been there for me. Saw me through all kinds of ridiculous drama with idiots in the lifestyle. And we've had some good times, too."

He gently traced her jaw with one hand, and snatched another tissue out of the box to dab at her tears with the other. "And there's no denying that the attraction between you and I has always been there, just kind of buzzing beneath the surface."

She blew her nose and took a bite of bacon. How did he make perfect bacon but manage to burn water? Solie sipped a bit more coffee, and then offered him the cup.

She felt all kinds of special when he took it, gulped without hesitation and set it down with a smile.

"While you're healing from your relationship with Wonder Dick, I hope to have a chance to play with you, then perhaps be more."

"Wonder Dick?" Solie snarfed her coffee and started coughing. Burt just shook his head at her and pounded her on her back.

"As I was saying, when you're ready, I want to talk about where this zing thing between us could go. What we could possibly grow to be to each other. So think about it, Solie?"

"But, but I have cooties!" she wailed. She never wailed…except for last night…in Burton's arms after learning about just how deep Marcais' dishonesty went. She'd been so upset that Mac fed her coconut brownies after dinner. Okay, so maybe she did occasionally wail. Whatever.

Burton looked at her with a mix of compassion and anger. "Luckily the cooties he gave you are curable. You had your massive dose of antibiotics yesterday. Seven days of no sex and you're good."

She knew this, but still she felt…tainted. Unclean. She tested clean before *and* after being with Marcais. In fact, he'd shown her his paperwork, so she knew he'd tested clean, too. So for him to give her an STI now meant he'd picked it up outside of their relationship. Obviously.

"Solie, stop it. I know what you're thinking."

"I thought you said you couldn't read minds," she snapped.

"Really?" he growled as he gave her "that look". She rolled her eyes and mumbled an apology.

"You did everything you were supposed to do, Solie. You're not at fault here. If you'd been the one slinging your pussy around to any and every one without protection, then yes, I'd blame you for this. But you didn't. That's all on him. I can't tell you not to feel angry or hurt, but I can remind you that this is not your fault. And it doesn't change how I feel about you."

She didn't say anything. Couldn't form the words past the lump in her throat.

"Do you hear me, Solie?"

She lifted her chin and looked at Burton as she had so many times over the years. Even while baring the most vulnerable parts of himself, the man was still a force of nature. Right now, Solie drew on that special energy of his and let it settle into herself. Chest loosened, upper lip stiffened and suddenly it was as if the tears of last night, and the sniffles of three minutes ago never existed.

Strength. It's what he gave her. Though she had plenty of her own, this was a different kind of fortitude. This wasn't boardroom-politics strength. This was more of a weather-a-shredded-heart kind of determination. She was more intimidated right now in her pj's trying to fathom letting her guard down the tiniest bit to let Burton in, than she would be if she were standing toe-to-toe with someone who threatened to take over her company.

He was in no way asking for all of her—not her heart, and perhaps not even her body. She knew that BDSM play wasn't all about sex with Burton. Sure, he enjoyed impact play with floggers, crops, rope and cuffs; however, what he loved most was getting into his play partner's head. And still, he hadn't even asked for that.

He'd only asked to give her what she needed…and she would be the one to decide what that was. And later, if she wanted to, he was open to moving into something a bit more…personal.

Slipping her hand into Burton's, Solie said exactly what was on her mind.

"Burt, I don't need to think about it."

"What are you saying, Solie," he asked with quiet surety. "No beating around the bush. Just let me have it."

"I want to explore this zing between us, B. And I'm ready to explore it now. Yes, I will admit I'm on the rebound, but we both know that. And right now, I want you more than anything or anyone else I can think of."

"More than a new souped-up gaming computer?" he teased, poking at her nerdy side.

"That's kind of pushing it, but yes, more than a new gaming computer. And more than World of WarCraft. And more than non-burnt English muffins. I want to be with you more than I want a bare handed, over the knee spanking."

"Now that's hard to believe," he quipped back. "But I think we can do something about that. Last I heard, there was nothing like a spanking from Mr. Big Thuddy Paddle Hands."

Solie's mouth fell open. "Mac told you about that?"

"Of course she did. And she had no shame in admitting that she's the one who came up with that loving little title for me while you wholeheartedly agreed. So I'll take that as a compliment."

Solie fell backwards onto her pillow laughing like she hadn't in weeks…hell, months even. She could tell Burton was seriously restraining himself from tickling her. When she caught her breath, she sat back up and smiled as he fed her more bacon.

"So what's the next step, Burt?"

"That depends. What do you want? I may be a Dominant, but I'm not a bully. You set the tone and the pace here, Sols. After that last D.I.N.O.—"

"D.I.N.O.? What's a D.I.N.O.?"

"Dominant-In-Name-Only."

"Oh." She chuckled and rolled her eyes. Didn't that about sum it up?

"Neither of us are into casual dating, but after *he who must not be named*, you may not even want a D/s dynamic, hon. And this may sound fucked up, but I want you happy, even if it's not with me. I can give you what you need until you decide that what you need isn't me."

"Not want a D/s dynamic? Oh, I definitely want it, Burt. I need it, actually. That's part of why that last thing was so disappointing and destructive. He knew what I needed, but his narcissism was more important. And now that I understand sociopaths, I get that it wasn't personal. Hey, did you know that he was actually convicted of domestic violence while we were living together?"

"What the fuck, Solie?!"

"Hey, I just found out myself. I knew he was going back and forth to court for some stuff with his ex-wife, but I thought it was simple post-divorce proceedings. He kept all the nasty details to himself. Straight up lied, actually."

"So he was living with you, was going back and forth to court for ex-wife stuff and ended up convicted? Fucking convicted, Solie? For domestic violence against…who? The ex?"

"Yep. And she's terrified of him, Burt."

"Damn. Talk about bullet dodged, woman. Given how aggressive he could be sometimes, and the way he would get up in your face and yell, it could have easily been you pressing charges against him, love."

"No doubt. But he wasn't stupid in that regard." Solie

was trained in two different martial arts, plus was proficient with firearms. Hell, she even had a hunter's license and could bag a fully grown elk at two hundred yards. "But back to the question you asked me about next steps. I think the next step is to determine what kind of relationship we want. I want to negotiate, set boundaries and all that, but even still, I want to take it one day at a time. And most important, I want you to be who you are, Burt. And that's alpha to the bone. And I'm not afraid of where that will lead because I know you, and alpha doesn't mean jerk in the Book of Burt."

"Book of Burt? I like that. We should also discuss triggers and things that might set you off given your recent ordeal. I don't want you walking on eggshells and I don't want to tip toe around either. Okay?"

Then Solie got up on her knees and did something she'd never done in all the time she'd known this man—she kissed Burton Khrys. And she put all her hopes, fears and desires into it as if her life depended on it.

* * * * *

He tasted of coffee and his own distinct flavor of pure man—a mix of strength and spicy heat that she hadn't realized she'd been dying to sample…until now.

But Burton didn't sample. He feasted.

One moment she was on her knees pressing her lips to his, and the next she was dragged into his lap and positioned to his liking. He held her tight as he slanted his mouth over hers. She felt the flex of muscle against her body as his arms tightened and released around her.

Suddenly he was pouring himself into the kiss, taking, plundering. She couldn't breathe. Didn't want to.

God, it was like drinking from a bottle of her favorite champagne after it had been shaken, uncorked and then pressed to her lips.

She opened to him. Held nothing back. Let him take what he wished. His tongue tangled with hers—not so much that she felt like she would gag, but just enough to make her want to chase him for more.

Burton pulled back just a bit.

"Let your head fall back, Solie."

She instantly obeyed, trusting him to keep her from tumbling off his lap and onto the floor. The second her neck went limp, Burton groaned his appreciation. And the sound was so deep, so masculine it made Solie's thighs quiver—thighs that happened to be pressed against his as she straddled his groin.

Kissed her neck. Nipped her jaw just enough to make her hiss. The bit of sting made her nibble on her own lips in anticipation of what he would do next.

He broke the kiss and whispered quietly into her ear.

"Tell me what you need."

"Hair," she gasped.

His fingers eased into her hair, to glide across the scalp and play with her locs. The gentle press of his fingertips was sweet followed by an exquisite bite of pain as he gathered a hank of it in his hand and squeezed. Hard.

Her hair, bundled in his hands as if his fingers were a scrunchy, reminded her of the man himself—tightly controlled, bundled strength.

Then thought faded away completely as she sank deeper into the kiss, further under this soul-satisfying spell, to *feel* rather than wonder at it all.

"What else, Sols? Now."

Without hesitation, the words tumbled from her lips between thick gasps. "Bite me. Please."

"Where?"

"Here." She touched the spot just beneath her ear and slid her fingers down her neck to a certain spot on just shy of her shoulder.

"Cross your arms behind your back and hold your elbows."

The moment she did, Burton yanked her head sideways and then nibbled along the path that her fingers had shown him. Suddenly his teeth sank into the muscle between neck and shoulder and Solie's eyes rolled back into her head.

"Oh my God," she gasped.

It was her sweet spot—the one place on her upper body where sensation could drive her to the brink of orgasm.

Fingers tightened even more at her scalp as he began to suck earnestly. Then he was biting again, then sucking. And all she could think of was…more.

He didn't try to touch her anywhere else, but focused only on what she'd said she needed. The sting of scalp and skin, mixed with the intimacy of his lips on hers was indescribably delicious.

And Solie was quickly heating up to a point where this bit of play wasn't enough.

Her hips went wild and there was nothing she could do to control them. The thick ridge of his cock pressed against her core, made her squirm and pant as he continued to bite her neck. Gasps became moans. Moans became cries. Cries became pleas.

She wasn't sure what she begged for, but whatever it was, only Burton could deliver it.

Lips left her skin and when Burt spoke Solie was pleased to hear he was just as winded as she was.

"I do believe kissing you has made my day, and it's only seven o'clock in the morning," he said. "But no sex. Not yet."

Solie started to withdraw, to sink down into a pool of disappointment as she was reminded of the sexually transmitted infection she'd been treated for just yesterday. But Burton Khrys wouldn't let her pull away.

"No sex, but not only because of your condition, Solie. I don't want to move too fast or rush you in any way. Understand?"

His consideration ramped her right back up to boiling. Arms twined around his neck, she held on for dear life. Solie's ears heard the words, but her brain wasn't processing them.

"Sols, I need to go. We'll finish this later."

But she was dialed up and eager. She ground her Hello Kitty jammy bottoms against his cock, reached for the little bit of sensation that would take her over the edge. She could come without sex, right? Hell yes! All she needed was just a little bit more. Just…

"Solie Alise Shaw." Uh oh. No one but her grandmother said her entire name, and only if she was in trouble.

Burt sank his fingers into her thigh with just enough pressure to deliver his message without actually hurting her. Solie stilled immediately.

"You're not speaking, but I'm not missing a single thing that your eyes or your sexy and oh-so-tempting body are saying. We will talk this out Solie. Starting tonight. You game?"

Game? Hell yes. She nodded her agreement.

"Use your words, Solie. Are you game?"

"Yes."

"Meet me at Twilight this evening. No working late for you. Six thirty sharp."

"Okay." He stood up with her still in his lap, then turned and eased back into bed. Head on his chest, Solie relaxed under gentle strokes that calmed and brought her down from that brink of delicious madness.

They shared the rest of the jumbo mug of coffee along with some comfortable small talk. Burt grabbed the remote off the nightstand and Solie found herself sharing a very "normal" morning with her friend as they watched the day's weather forecast on TV.

A few minutes later, a sexy, nicely caffeinated Burton climbed out of bed and pressed a kiss to her forehead.

His gaze took her all in as he said, "I'm all yours as of this moment, Sols."

She gawked as he grinned at her and backed into her bathroom. A few minutes later he was dressed and gone, and Solie headed into a scalding hot shower.

Her whole body hummed—every spot he'd touched and even the ones he hadn't. It was as if her very blood shimmered beneath the skin.

For a woman who managed a corporation on a daily basis and planned damn near everything to the nth degree, this thing with Burt she hadn't seen coming.

She moaned aloud as the water sluiced over the bruises forming on her neck where Burton had been so very thorough. It was tender to the touch and the thought made Solie smile like a loon.

She looked up at the ceiling, watched the steam swirl around as it rose. Then she let out the elation bubbling in her gut as she screamed, "Oh my God, I haz a boyfriend! Burton Khrys is mine! Wheeee!"

She twirled until she almost fell and busted her ass on the slick tiles. And even then, Solie couldn't stop the wild grin from spreading across her lips, nor the flash of anticipation from dancing around in her belly.

And she didn't want to control it. Not in the slightest.

CHAPTER FOUR

"*Konbanwa*. Welcome to Twilight Teahouse. Would you please confirm your preference for this evening, Miss Solie?"

Solie beamed and executed a formal bow. "Yes, thank you, Kuri. I'll be having both dinner and dessert." She didn't bother asking about a reservation, knowing that Burton would have seen to it if he'd told her to be here.

"Wonderful, Miss Solie. Please wait here. Your table is almost ready. Mina will be along to escort you in a moment."

"*Arigato gozaimasu*," Solie replied, thanking her hostess in perfect Japanese.

Kuri bowed and then turned to greet other guests. Her traditional kimono was a gentle swish of purple silk covered with delicate-looking cherry blossoms. Solie was always amazed at how every attendant always had every single hair in place and perfectly coifed. Elegance and class with a dose of kink described Twilight Teahouse perfectly.

For dinner she'd have a shrimp salad and fresh

yellowtail sashimi. If she was brave enough, dessert, would be the St. Andrew's cross in the far corner of the play space upstairs in the Hall of Mirrors.

Yes, this place had become her personal crack. Japanese teahouse in the front, and a world-class, well-equipped, totally not-somebody's-converted-basement dungeon on the upper floors.

As she stood in the waiting area, Solie looked around. Being here once again brought a mix of giddy anticipation and inner-growly annoyance.

The last time she'd played here was when one of the area's premier rope Tops had agreed to give Marcais flogging and rope lessons as a favor to Solie. That Friday night, Solie had gladly been both the rope bunny and the flog bunny.

Even now, the details of that time started out bright and shiny in her memory, then unrolled themselves like a stained cheap carpet.

The play had been fabulous. In fact, she and Marcais had gone home and played some more that night, and then did yet another scene on Saturday morning. It had been a wonderful way to begin a weekend and each session had gone just the way she'd hoped. The buzz-like floaty experience had been followed by standing in front of the mirror and admiring the pretty deep purple marks left on her skin.

A smile played over her lips as she recalled Mac's words—*"Solie, you look like a cinnamon tiger with a rainbow-striped ass!"*

But then Sunday rolled around and Solie had hit bottom. Hard.

Just as one sometimes experienced subspace, or endorphin rushes, after heavy impact play, Solie found herself living the polar opposite—an endorphin crash, or sub-drop. And she'd "dropped" so deeply into a funky depression, she'd wanted to stick her head out the window and slam it closed on the back of her neck. It was like falling down a deep pit full of spikes...and just never getting to the spikes. When she'd tried to call Marcais, he'd been incognito. Gone. Dropped off the face of the planet. Wouldn't answer his phone nor return her texts.

By evening, she'd hit full-blown subby distress, and was completely out of chocolate, damn it. Thank God for Mac and Burt. Those two had come over to keep her company and both were livid by the time Marcais finally got back to her late that night. And Burton was beyond pissed, had even snatched the phone and torn Marcais a new one after Marcais had finally admitted that he didn't know what sub-drop was, hence his lack of urgency in getting back to her.

Solie had been amazed. Marcais was the first to ever get her to a place where subspace bliss had occurred. So he was also the first she'd experienced sub-drop with. And though it had been her first sub-drop, she'd at least known what the hell was happening to her and why.

How did a person just tool around in this lifestyle and not bother to learn how their actions could physically affect the person they Topped? And how had he hidden something so significant as his lack of knowledge for so long?

He'd lied. Skillfully and often.

Just...goddammit.

As the memory rolled through her, Solie recalled her reaction when she'd learned that while she'd been in sub-drop hell, her so-called Dominant had been chatting up one of the attendants right here at the Teahouse. While trying to talk the woman into having coffee with him, he'd used the same cheesy line he'd used on Solie when they'd first met.

"Are you single or am I too late?"

Yeah, that.

She hated the memories of it all, hated that it flashed into her brain as she stood at the threshold of the Twilight Teahouse's inner sanctum awaiting the man of her fucking dreams. It had only been a month since what felt like the ultimate heartbreak by a world class man-whore, yet a part of her felt like she should be further along. Instead, it was all still so very fresh in her mind.

Usually she liked fresh things.

But this? Not so much.

Solie knew herself. Knew exactly where she stood in regard to her emotional and psychological recovery—she had a long way to go in the mending process. And a trip to the Twilight Teahouse with Burton was the ticket. Or at least the beginning.

Right then, one of Solie's favorite service Tops rolled in looking like a decadent breath of fresh air. Rachelle served others by Topping them in the manner they required, and she was damn good at it. Handing her large black duffel off to one of the male attendants, the woman made a beeline for Solie.

Arms spread wide, she said, "Ah, So-leee, how are jew daaahling? So vunderful to see jew!" The words were full of joy and wrapped in Rachelle's smooth French accent as she pulled Solie into a fierce hug.

Solie grinned and tried to answer, but her face was smashed between the taller woman's breasts. So instead, she simply inhaled Rachelle's floral light perfume and let the comradery flow over her. After all, the woman offered to castrate Marcais if he ever showed his face at the TT again. Yes, it was good to be back here for sure.

No surprise that Rachelle knew what Marcais had done. In fact, it may as well have been on the local news considering how many women had come forward after word of his trifling behavior had gone viral. There were too many to count that had either been approached by him or had slept with him. And yes, they'd known about

Solie, but Solie hadn't known about any of them.

"Well, I knew he was seeing some people, but I was seeing some people too, so I didn't really think much of it."

Which basically meant that that particular bitch hadn't cared that Marcais was cheating on Solie and had been happy to be "the other woman". Another had claimed that she and Marcais had fallen so hard for each other and she just loved him so much, and blah, blah, blah.

Solie hugged Rachelle back as the other woman kissed each cheek and offered some slow-motion castration for Marcais. One thing was certain—good friends with encouraging words, cuddles and chocolate were greatly appreciated at times like this. Take those same friends and add floggers and the occasional paddle, and you had a total god-send.

Rachelle was skipping dinner tonight and headed directly to one of the banks of private elevators strictly for club members. Moments later she was greeted by yet another club regular, and another.

Perhaps Mac and Burton were right and she'd truly been missed in the local community?

As if conjured, Burton's big warm hand slipped around her waist.

She turned her head to meet the gaze of the one of the most darkly gorgeous men on planet Earth. And he happened to be grinning at her as if he'd won the lottery. Perhaps, in his mind, he had.

Body heat radiated through his clothes as he pressed close to her from behind, wrapped his arms around her, and placed a soft kiss on her check.

"Good evening, beautiful. I love this dress on you," he whispered in her ear as he discretely traipsed a finger up the spine exposed by the knee-length red and black backless number.

"I'm glad you like it." Lord, she was almost breathless just from that simple touch; as this morning's kisses replayed themselves over again in her mind. Oh man, she had it bad. "You gave it to me for Christmas last year, and Mac gave me the matching shoes."

He looked down at her feet to the red suede heels, and when his gaze once again met hers, it smoldered until she was sure her panties would catch fire. She'd seen that look before, but it had never been directed at her.

Burton moved deeper into her personal space, and was almost lip-to-lip when he said, "Baby, those shoes are meant to be airborne. Damn, we have good taste."

And they did indeed considering he was dressed impeccably. Black slacks and a black silk pullover knit sweater set off his mesmerizing blues until they shone like jewels. Dark, hard, and a twinkle of a smile made this man number one on the delish list.

Having Burt's full attention did funny things to her organs—the damn things just seemed to dance all over the place. And after the recent hell she'd been through, she was happy to let them do the mambo if they wanted to. Why? Because there was one thing she knew— Burton was sincere. If he'd been anything over the years, it was honest. Sometimes brutally so.

There was quite a line waiting to be seated by the time their attendant arrived a few minutes later.

"Good evening, Miss Solie," Mina said. Then she turned to Burt with the same graceful bow and said, "Master Burton."

"Good evening, Mina. Thank you for seeing to us this evening." Burton bowed, then took Mina's hand and planted a chaste kiss. Solie hid a smile as the hostess blushed and giggled, a bit flustered and put out as she motioned for them to follow her.

As they were led down the silk-lined hallway and through the thick double doors into the dining area, Solie wondered why it felt so new. She'd been down these same hallways a bazillion times; eaten and played here, even danced and partied here plenty. But tonight, in this moment, it felt…

She took in a deep breath as the light bulb went on. This was a new chapter in her life, and who better to accompany her on a new journey than an old friend?

As they walked, Burt's hand settled on her lower back and her stomach dove down into the soles of her feet.

Wow. Tummy wiggles and goose bumps? Heh.

"What are you smiling at, Sols? Looks like you have a secret."

"Oh, nothing," she lied. Burt's raised brow let her know that he wasn't buying it, but he was obviously letting her get away with it…for now.

Once through the main dining-room doors, they stopped at the shoe station, slipped off their shoes and placed them in the little wooden bin with their table number on it. Twilight Teahouse provided traditional tabi socks or slippers for each guest. Tonight Solie chose a pair that matched her dress. Burt followed suit and chose a gray pair of men's slippers.

The slippers were so comfortable, Solie almost didn't look forward to getting her own shoes back.

Shoji screens separated each booth, where classily dressed people sat and enjoyed their meals. Candlelight cast a romantic glow off the highly polished wooden table tops. The aroma of various teas filled the air, complimenting the scents from the dishes that were being delivered to those who were dining.

Once at their table, Solie automatically slid into the booth, but not before Burton pressed the sweetest kiss to her lips—a kiss that finished the story his eyes had begun to tell when they met up in the lobby only moments before. It was a tale of possibilities. Very, very good ones.

They made small talk about their day until the waiter arrived with tea…and no menu. With a bow and a smile, he turned and left.

Solie looked after him wondering why he hadn't bothered to take her order. She was dying for some fresh Ahi, damn it. She opened her mouth to call him back, then snapped it shut at Burt's word.

"Don't worry. I ordered ahead."

Her pissy side reared its head, but she smacked it back down. She knew what she was getting into the moment she'd accepted his offer this morning. Or at least she *thought* she knew.

Besides, this wasn't anything new. Burton liked to order the food for their table. Always had. Even Mac occasionally let him get away with it and that woman didn't have a submissive bone in her body.

"Stop glaring at me and take your meds, Solie. Dinner will be here pretty quickly."

She didn't stop glaring, but she did do as he asked and fished her diabetes medicine out of her purse and gulped it down with some tea.

He took a sip of water and sat back even as she leaned forward with her arms crossed on the table. The shift in their relationship dynamic was swift and had her tilting her head at a hard right. Add hunger to the mix and you had a less-than-giddy Solie.

"I thought we were going to talk tonight." Oooh, she hadn't meant to snarl, but she was hungry, damn it.

Like some people were unpleasant drunks, Solie was an unhappy hungry person. In her head, she was like the little old lady she'd seen in a movie. The woman sat waiting for her lunch while her waiter talked on the phone, laughed and cracked jokes with whoever was on the other end. Meanwhile the lady, who was also diabetic, sat and waited. And waited. And waited some more. Finally she'd tossed aside the entire table, yelled, "Where is my food?!", and then chased the waiter around the restaurant and finally out the front door.

"And we will talk. After we eat." He gave her a moment of silence and simply watched. Too closely. "Are you having second thoughts about being with me? As a friend, I know I can be somewhat bossy."

She almost choked and snarfed water through her nose. *Somewhat* bossy? Really?

"As a lover," he continued, "I am even more demanding. But it will work for you."

"Really? And why is that?" she asked. A bit of growl still laced the words though she was trying hard to get her hunger-induced annoyance under control.

"Because what you really crave is to be in service to someone. Don't interrupt, Solie." She snapped her mouth shut and reached for the tea pot as if that's what she'd meant to do all along. She poured quickly and then lifted the small traditional cup to her lips.

It was so hot she almost burned her mouth off, but no way she'd let him know by yowling.

"As I was saying, you wish to be in service to someone. But to someone who not only appreciates all that you do, but who gives you a reason to continue doing it. For example, that time when Marcais needed work done on his truck, but the dumbass had no idea how to handle it. You did the research and took care of it. Not because you're a control freak, but because that's what he needed."

Truth. And nothing but.

"However, he hadn't appreciated it. Gave you no reason to continue serving him. I remember that you saved his grown ass several times because of his own stupidity. Bottom line is Solie, he lost your respect a long time ago. He may have known his way around a spanking, but he didn't know *you*, the woman."

She had nothing to say to that. Couldn't find a single thing to dispute…and she was trying really, *really* hard to think of something redeeming about that whole situation. Other than Marcais delivering some really good sex, nothing came to mind.

How depressing.

Thankfully she didn't have to reply because dinner arrived quickly, just as Burton promised.

And he'd ordered her favorites. All of them.

By the time she was done stuffing her face, she'd inhaled what must have surely been a bucket-full of fresh Ahi, salmon, yellow tail and prawns, a trough of wakame seaweed salad, and enough pickled mango, wasabi and ginger for ten people. She wasn't one of those women who didn't eat when out on a date. In fact, she still had a bit of room and would have kept right on going if Burton hadn't reminded her that dessert was still forthcoming.

As soon as the dishes were cleared, Mina returned.

"Where would you like your dessert served, Master Burton? There are open seats on floor one off to the right of the ankle stocks, and another on the small loveseat near the spanking bench."

"Which spanking bench?" Solie asked.

"The burgundy leather one, ma'am. If you prefer some privacy, the bamboo room is also free."

Her stomach did a free fall at the thought of being alone with Burt in the bamboo room. There was absolutely nothing in there but a huge beanbag-like chair big enough for literally five people. The reason it was called the bamboo room was because the door that led inside was made of bamboo poles and you could see right inside.

She'd never taken advantage of that particular space

before, other than when invited to watch others indulge. She pictured herself laying in Burt's arms in a cuddle puddle and felt her cheeks heat. But not because she was embarrassed at all, but because the thought of all that solid flesh pressed against her set a fire down south that might require an extinguisher.

Suddenly an image of Burton dressed like a firefighter popped into her head.

Pulling her mind out of the proverbial gutter, Solie turned to Burt.

He was looking at her as if he knew exactly what she was thinking. Her breathing hitched. Burt's eyes lit up like Christmas trees. A subtle, but very *there* smile tilted up one side of his mouth. Guess she hadn't been successful in hiding her reaction over such a little thing as picking a spot for dessert.

She cleared her throat and asked, "Do you have a preference as to where we have dessert?"

His words and tone were totally smooth when he replied, "Not really. You choose."

And just like that his gaze had her pinned in place. Did he really want her to choose, or was he waiting to see if she would defer to him? It wasn't something she typically worried about with Burton, but it was a game Marcais played. Often.

Burt tilted his head. "Solie, you okay, hon?"

Ripping her gaze away from his deep blues, she simply said, "Yes, I'm fine. Up to you. Lead the way please."

And she refused to look at him again until they were seated next to each other near one of the stations where an expert flogger was using a Florentine double-handed technique. He was very smooth and practiced, almost like a martial artist demonstrating how to use a staff or bo. The result of his flogging was even stripes on the back of the women who held onto a pair of large thick rings.

Her arms and legs were spread. Fingers wrapped around the steel attached to the top of the wooden structure. She wasn't tied or secured in any way, her partner trusting her to keep her fingers exactly where they were.

Their dessert arrived just as the strokes began to fall a bit faster and harder. The volume of the woman's moans, quiet and barely there at first, rose with the intensity of the strikes.

A part of Solie wanted to be the woman on the receiving end of the flogging. Part of her resented that she wasn't that woman because the man who should be flogging her was surely laying up with yet another woman by now. Then she felt guilty because she was thinking about the former dude rather than the man sharing her dessert right here, right now.

"Okay, tell me what's going on." The words were quietly spoken, but were clearly nothing short of an order, given the steel infused in them.

"What?" she asked.

"You went weird on me after I gave you the choice of where we would have dessert. Tell me."

Shit. So much for wishing he'd missed that.

She took in a deep breath and looked Burton right in the eye. All she could do was suck it up and be honest. So she told him how she'd slipped back into Marcais-induced behavior, wondering if Burt really wanted her to pick, or if he was just looking for a reason to start a fight and be a dick.

"Are you mad?" she asked.

"Can't be. That's where you are right now. And if I'm any kind of a man I have to meet you where you are, not where I want you to be. I told you this morning that I knew you were in the early stages of getting over all this madness and I'm willing to be what you need. Luckily, what you need is a mean old man. I've got you covered."

Oh good grief. She snorted a laugh.

"So, tell me about the phone call from *he who must not be named's* commanding officer."

Saved by Burt's intuition on when to change a subject. She wished she had the man's gift. But on the other hand, no one was perfect considering Burt had also had his fill of dealing with cuh-ray-zee.

"Marcais' First Sergeant walked into his office in front of all his co-workers, made him stop what he was doing, and escorted him directly to the medical facility. He was tested and treated on the spot."

Burt whistled and then grinned like a loon. "Back to that whole karma thing, right? I told you this guy should have been Sméagol."

Solie looked up at the server and murmured her thanks as a crystal mug of hot tea was set down on their small table. "Smee-who?"

"You know, Sméagol from the Lord of the Rings." Then in a completely terrible accent, he said, "I told you he was tricksy. I told you he was false. Stupid fat hobbit!"

They both laughed until she was damn near out of breath.

Finally Burt said, "Now, on to us."

She cleared her throat and jumped in with both feet.

"Okay. I want to put this out there now, up front. After a while…" She paused, took a sip of tea for fortification—this time it wasn't lava-lip-burning hot—and then laid out her one true desire. "If our relationship is working the way we want, I want a collar out of this deal."

She watched the blood drain from his face. But she was proud of herself for not taking it personally. Solie knew exactly what was going through the man's mind. The last woman he'd given his collar to was supposed to become his wife. Burton Khrys didn't play around when it came to intimate relationships. When he realized that regardless of what he did, said or gave, he just wasn't what that woman needed, he'd ended it. Tore his heart out in the process.

But Solie wasn't going to be less than honest. She was tired of trying relationships on for size with open-ended expectations. She wanted something permanent with someone she was compatible with.

"Well," she said, "looks like you're the one that needs to give it some thought, eh?" she said with her typical sass.

"Smart ass," he grumbled.

"Damn right."

"You know you're going to pay for that at some point right?"

"Of course I do." But they hadn't negotiated anything yet, so she knew it was safe to be as much of a brat as she wanted. It felt damn good considering she typically spent her days being a hard ass. *Not* being in control, *not* making all the decisions was like a refreshing cool breeze on a hot summer day to her. And right now, she was basking in it.

"Let's get the negotiations out of the way. I'm suddenly eager to get started," Burt said.

Out of the blue, Mac appeared and sat down with them.

"Am I late?"

"Late for what?" Solie asked before the shock could truly register.

"I, my dear girl, am going to mediate your negotiation with Mr. Thuddy here."

"Excuse me?" Solie gasped.

"Not forever. Just for tonight," Mac clarified.

Burt grinned until Solie was sure she saw little horns start growing out of his forehead as he said, "Let the games begin."

* * * * *

The negotiations went smoothly as they both laid out what they would and wouldn't tolerate as they explored this new facet of an old relationship. As soon as limits were set, Landon walked over. The whole crew smiled her way as Mac's husband sat an oversized piece of seven layer chocolate decadence in front of her, along with a steaming hot pot of aromatic jasmine tea.

Being surrounded by people who cared for her made Solie feel as if the sun had risen over her little spot at the table. She knew this was a safe place where she could say any and everything, and it would remain in confidence.

"So what's your poison tonight?" Mac asked with a fairly wicked grin.

With a tired sigh, Solie simply replied, "Nothing."

Mac took both her hands while Burton sat back and let the moment happen. Energy hummed off of him and she knew he was up to something. The man was so good at being unobtrusive yet bossy at the same time. And how did he manage to pull that off, anyway?

"Solie, listen, you can't be so hard on yourself," Mac said as Landon handed her a fork and poured her tea as his wife tried to set her straight. "There's no way you could have known what he was. Sociopaths are experts at concealing the truth. Pros at charming people out of anything and everything. For them there's no empathy. It's not about emotions. It's about winning."

"But I think I did know. I just didn't stop long enough to really analyze what I was seeing, hearing and feeling. Instead I just went ahead and jumped into it, choosing to believe him rather than stepping back to think for a minute."

"Well, you know, or rather you know *now*, that sociopaths move in fast. They push the relationships quickly for a reason—while they're laying on the charm and manipulating you, they get you addicted to their special kind of attention. You're in it before you know what hit you. I mean, look at the other women who've come forward. And the one that's still involved with him, even though she knows she was his little secret."

"It doesn't change the fact that he pretty much told me what he was and I walked into the shit anyway."

Burt sat forward now, humming with an energy that was a bit more on the darker side. Edgy. And focused. "Solie, what are you saying?" he asked in that super calm voice of his—the one that *sounded* nonchalant but was deadly serious and no-nonsense to boot.

"I'll tell you like I told Marcais. He once told me that his ex-wife hated his flirting, but he kept right on doing it. His wife was the woman he was supposed to love, cherish and protect more than anything. And if he didn't stop flirting for her, what the hell made me think he would do it for me? He told me that he used to lie to his wife about everything, and I mean everything about himself. So if he lied to her, a woman he was with for eight years, why would he tell me the fucking truth?

Mac's eyes went wide in surprise. "Wow, you dropped an F-bomb? In public? All righty then."

Solie let the words continue to rush out. "He once even told me I was expendable."

"What?! I'll kill him."

"No, that's not what I mean, Mac. And sit down and eat some more cake, woman.

Anyway, he once told me that the way to get over one woman was to get another one. Well, he basically all but told me that I was nothing but a distraction to help him get over his ex-wife. And whenever I asked him about his feelings for me, his answer was, 'Well, I don't know you yet.' Yeah, that's key for, 'I don't have deep feelings for you, Solie.' What's worse is that he would tell me that his co-workers at the Army base would ask him where he always found so many quality women. But he'd only been divorced for a few months when he and I got together. So when did he have time to find all these girls?"

"I see what you're saying."

"I knew you'd get it. He was either messing around on his wife, which she confirmed he did for eight years, or he was messing with a bunch of women while he was scoping me out, which also turned out to be true. Basically, he waved some pretty big red flags in front of my face, and I was so caught up in his charm, I didn't see them."

"I see what you mean. But knowing it wasn't personal should make that particular pill a bit easier to swallow."

"True, but it's still a bitter pill, you guys. Cod liver oil mixed with crushed aspirin bitter. I mean, *dayum*."

Burton rose to his imposing height and held out his hand to her. "Well, if you'd like a bit of medicine that's a tad bit sweeter, come on up to the third floor. I think I have something you might appreciate."

"Should I be scared?"

"It's me we're talking about here, Solie," Burton said in mock outrage.

"Yep, scared. Definitely scared," she said, voice deadpan with mock fear. She even threw in a little shaking and wiping of non-existent tears from her eyes. Inside, she squirmed, wondered if he would ask…no. He wouldn't ask. Had no need to.

Negotiations were done. It had taken next to no time. In fact, he'd simply slid a piece of paper across the table right after Mac had shown up. Listed were the things he believed would be hard limits for her. He'd hit them all dead on, except for one—and that's because while it might have been a no-go with others, she trusted Burton to introduce her to edge play in a way that wouldn't break her.

She glanced over at Burt and caught him and Mac passing a certain look.

"What are you two up to?"

"Do you trust me, Sols?" Burt asked. Forced herself to relax though inside she squirmed, anxious to experience what Burton would do to her. All she had to do…was say yes.

"Of course."

"Then finish your dessert and head up to the Ice Palace. Five minutes." He took her hand and kissed it, keeping his eyes on hers the entire time. Then he turned and walked the hell away.

Mac sat there and sang a song she called "Ode to Mr. Thuddy Paddle Hands" while grinning like a nutball. Solie wanted to smash what was left of her chocolate decadence into her friend's nose. Instead she took her time finishing her yummies and dallied. Well, she dallied as close to five minutes as she could with just enough time to grab her heels from the shoe bin and book it upstairs.

* * * * *

The proprietor who'd dreamed up Twilight Teahouse was brilliant. The entire five-story club was private, except for the restaurant. Solie had inhaled a perfect dinner on the public side of the first floor, and a delectable dessert on the private side. The second floor held a full-service spa, complete with traditional Japanese baths and massage space.

Each floor had its own particular theme, from hot Egyptian nights to sultry Caribbean days. But now, it was time for the icing on her particular cake—The Ice Palace on the third floor, Solie's absolute favorite.

As the elevator moved, she held her own gaze in the mirrored walls. This morning after Burton had left her, she'd washed and braided her hair. Once dry, she took it down to reveal a mop of glossy, dark brown, wavy locs that swung with health every time she turned her head. The bit of gloss she'd worn on her lips was long gone, courtesy of her chocolate dessert and a linen napkin. A touch of waterproof eyeliner finished her off. It was next to nothing in the makeup department, but she never wore much when coming here. It squicked her out to see other people's sweat, tears and makeup streaked over the furniture, so she made sure she didn't leave anything for anyone else to clean up.

Her brain zoned out at the thought of the many spray bottles of disinfectant and clean towels that dotted the place.

The elevator slowed and thoughts of Burton's handsome face pushed the squick from her mind. That edgy smile he'd given her along with his "you've got five minutes" declaration set a different kind of shiver skating over her skin.

"God, girl, you are in over your head." Funny thing was...she liked it. "Maybe you're just as nuts as Marcais?" Laughing at herself, she shook her head and smoothed down her already smooth dress.

Amazing how Burt set her to twitching. Solie stared down directors of multi-billion dollar companies every quarter when it was time for her vendor review, yet one arched eyebrow from Burton made her as nervous as a bug in a henhouse.

He looked at her just like that, too. Like he wanted to devour her.

"Yep. Definitely in over your head. And you're talking to yourself in an empty elevator while staring at your reflection in a mirror." So why the hell was she grinning like she'd just had a shot of pure endorphin right into her brain?

Humans. Such complex creatures. Surely they were the only animals on Earth that could be happy, excited and terrified all at the same time...and like it.

Sigh.

The elevator doors parted with a quiet swoosh. On the other side, Burton stood between her and the exit with an outstretched hand. He seemed to love holding hands. Interesting she hadn't noticed before. Even when watching his interactions with his ex, he'd never given off this "I want to snuggle" vibe before.

Hard ass mixed with cuddle puddle?

I think I can work with this.

They passed several stations with spanking benches and massage tables, and rooms that appeared to be wide open but could be closed off with screens or by simply sliding the embedded glass doors shut and drawing the curtains.

It was like tooling through a crystal palace in a science fiction movie. There weren't any scaly, green women up here, but endless white—white walls, white tiled floors and one-way glass. Secrets were safe within; even with all the lights on in the darkness of night, no one could see inside from the street.

Mirrored pillars topped with marble and crystal sculptures reflected light in a mix of rainbow-prism arcs and edges. Muted brilliance filled the room until you swore you were inside a sparkling masterpiece of ice, minus the bone-chilling cold.

A quick glance at her watch. It was still early, especially for a Monday night. No surprise that they passed no one as Burton led her to a semi-open space with three walls.

"In you go," he said quietly.

Solie took off her shoes. The tile of the walkway was cool against the soles of her feet as she stepped off the main floor and onto the carpet of their play room for the evening. It was almost completely empty. One wall had a number of D-rings and assorted attachments for ropes, cuffs and things. A dark blue, overstuffed chair provided the only splash of color; and looked like it would have been more at home in her living room in front of the big-screen TV. Off to the side was a long table covered with a white cloth. Burton stooped, dragged a huge black duffel out from underneath and set it on the table with a loud "thunk".

The thoughts in her head were mirthful. She'd seen this man in action, and every time she did it made her equal parts jealous and equal parts happy that she wasn't on the receiving end. Burton could indeed be a deliciously mean old man.

And it was what she wanted. Craved. God, she *needed*.

Gently, he put a hand on each cheek and kissed her. Then, fingers tensed on her jaw. Soft gentle touch morphed into a firm, unyielding grip. Enough to get her attention but not enough to bruise or cause true discomfort. Something flared in his gaze and Solie found herself facing an entirely different person. In the blink of an eye, this was another man—this was *the* Burton Khrys.

Uh, maybe I should start backing away. Slowly.

Too late.

"I want you to pick ten things out of this bag that you want me to use on you. Put them right here." He motioned to the table top. "Place them in order with the ones you're not quite sure of or want to try for the first time on the far left, and the ones you like most on the right."

She started to nod. Burton gave her the Mr. Spock

one-raised-eyebrow look.

Words, woman. Use your words. Funny she never had this problem with anyone but this guy. Solie opened her mouth with a simple, "Okay."

"Are you sure? If you're not ready, we can wait. I think you need this, but in the end you hold the control here…until you give it to me."

"I'm fine, it's just I'm not a big impact player like you are and I'm not sure if I can…"

He crowded into her space, cornered her with his big body.

"Baby, I can give you exactly what you need. I've got you, okay?" Suddenly she wanted to lower her gaze, look anywhere but at him. But before the thought could complete in her head, Burt lifted her chin with a single finger, looked deeply into her eyes. Captured her gaze until there was nowhere to go, nowhere to look, but right back at him.

Then the man pulled her close, wrapped her securely in his arms. Kissed the wind right out of her sails. Her response, instant and uncontrolled. Leaning in, she took all he had to offer with that mouth, those hands.

With each pass of his tongue against hers, Solie sank just a bit further into her need. Burton buried his fingers into her locs as he deepened the contact. He pulled gently. Tilted her head a bit to the left. Solie sighed into his mouth, loving that all she had to do was stand there and let him direct her where he wanted her to go.

Mmm. He tasted of chocolate decadence, coffee and a touch of mint. The flex of muscles in his arms ratcheted up her anxiousness. Not because she was afraid, but because she hadn't realized—or wanted to admit—just how much stress she'd been carrying around until she'd started to let go of some of it.

He pulled harder, just enough to cause her to gasp at the bit of sting at her scalp. A moan edged up out of her throat at the delicious trail of dampness left behind as Burton nibbled his way down one side of her neck and up the other.

By the time he reached her opposite ear, Solie was damn near panting.

Teeth tugged on an earring and then he whispered. "Strip. Keep the panties on. Ten minutes."

Once again he turned to leave, but not before he pulled a pair of shoji screens into position at the arched entranceway to give her some privacy.

She tossed her shoes off to the side. Must have had too much sugar given the way her fingers trembled as she undid the clasp at her neck that held up her dress.

A quiet tap on the screen.

"Sols, it's me. Can I come in?"

Mac.

"Of course." Solie turned, holding her dress up with one hand. "Whatcha up to? Doing a scene with Landon tonight?"

"Nope." Mac dropped Solie's personal play bag next to the blue cushy chair.

"First you appear to magically mediate negotiations and now you have my play bag? Woman, when the hell did you manage to get your hands on that?" Solie demanded. She knew exactly what was in that bag, and right now she wasn't sure how she felt about it.

Mac grinned and attempted to look innocent. She failed miserably.

"I stopped by your house on my way over here to drop off a casserole. This was sitting in the hallway all lonesome and such." She motioned to the royal blue and black designer bag on the floor while she dropped her ass into the chair. "Oh, I checked your back door, which you'd left unlocked by the way. And I fed your horse-sized dog, too."

Solie snorted and rolled her eyes. "And I did not

leave my door unlocked, and my German shepherd is supposed to be horse sized. The better to bite your backside with."

"Need help with that dress?"

"Nah." Solie paused. "You look awful comfy. You staying?"

"Yep. I'm your protector tonight, so I made sure to bring all the goodies."

Dress forgotten, it fell of completely and hit the floor as Solie braced her hands on her hips. Temper flared as she glared at her best friend. Understanding dawned in her mind —she'd been blessed…or something, with the two most caring, nosey ass people in the universe.

"And who the hell decided you were going to look after me while doing a scene? In fact, who said I was playing tonight at all?" Solie snapped.

"You did."

"Excuse me?"

Mac was up out of that chair and in Solie's face, standing toe to toe…or boots to toe. Whatever.

"You heard me, woman. You chose me as your protector the moment you said yes to Burton Khrys this morning!"

Solie's grumble became a growl. "He told you about that? What are you two, a couple of teenaged girls who talk on the phone at all hours of the night?"

"If being a teenaged girl means Burton cared enough to call me this morning to ask me to be here in case you needed me, then fuck yes, I'm a teenaged girl," MacKenzie snapped right back.

Really?

"Mac, you're a fucking mother hen, is what. Isn't it enough that you feed me several times a week, damn it?"

"You're my best friend, Solie Shaw. And I love you to pieces. And so what if I feed you several times a week? You're always working and it's what you need, damn it. Now move your ass. You're down to six minutes."

Aw hell. And she hadn't chosen a single thing out of Burton's stuffed-to-the-hilt bag.

Solie stepped out of the red and black fabric puddle. Mac swiped it up, walked her sexy ass back to the oversized chair and started pulling stuff out of Solie's personal bag. "I've got your fluffy blanket here for after, as well as some chocolate and plenty of water for you. So take care of your task. I've got the rest of this. Oh, and take off the jewelry, just in case."

Handing over her watch, earrings and necklace, Solie hustled over to Burt's bag and grabbed five things she was familiar with. The rest, she just guessed at their purpose and quickly laid them out on the table in the order she'd been instructed to.

"Nervous?" Mac asked. "Okay, never mind. I know that 'duh' look when I see it, Solie. We knew you'd be a bit nervous after your recent not-so-great experience and that's why Burt asked me to be here. Just to be reassurance for you. You know, a second set of eyes and ears."

"I appreciate it, Mac. I do. This is all just so intense and so very...I don't know." She sucked in a deep breath and tried to relax. It wasn't working so she did the next best thing—she changed the subject. "What I'd love is to watch you and Landon. It's been awhile since I've seen you two play."

Marcais hadn't ever wanted to come to the club on the same nights as her friends. She'd never noticed just how much he'd separated her from the people who cared about her. Controlled where she went and with whom. And so smoothly, Solie hadn't noticed until Mac mentioned it some months back.

But Solie had started paying very close attention and had been shocked at the corner she'd allowed herself to be manipulated into.

Then she'd gotten out. Fast.

Just not quite fast enough, damn it.

Some of the deepest wounds a person could inflict on another were the kind that were unseen—like words that cut to the bone. Solie only hoped she was strong enough, healed enough to choose to accept this chance to have who and what she really wanted.

Mac was her favorite kinky bitch on heels, and occasionally submitted to her husband in the sack. Yet as much as she admired her good friend, Solie didn't want what Mac had. She didn't want to Top her man. She didn't want to be in charge in the bedroom. Actually, she didn't want to be in charge at home, period. Running her office and all her consultants was enough, thank you verra much.

And speaking of "in charge", where the hell was Burton?

"Good grief, woman, will you stop pacing? Your boobs are very distracting bouncing around like that."

Solie rounded on her friend, but the expression on Mac's face brought her up short. The woman was sprawled, one leg over the arm of the big chair, with a huge teasing grin on her face. Busted. Solie was indeed pacing. Definitely not the norm for her, but it seemed her feet were trying to catch up with the fucking pterodactyls flipping around in her gut.

And why was she so nervous? This wasn't her first rodeo, after all. And she was going to be playing with a man she'd known for years and years. So…what was she so concerned about?

Perhaps she really was messed up in the head?

"No you're not," Burton said from the doorway.

Shit. Had she said that out loud?

"Yes, Solie. You said that out loud. Mac, give us a minute. I'll call you in when we're ready to get started."

Without a word, Mac nodded at Burton, winked at Solie and showed herself out.

Burton came fully into the room and for some reason, Solie couldn't meet his gaze. A part of her felt…diminished. Not quite herself. Unsure. Unsettled.

Unworthy.

Burton sat in the chair while she stood off to the side. Here she was, damn near naked, in a pair of red and black polka dot panties that showcased her body to perfection. Yet in her head, she stood at a wall with her face practically wedged in a corner.

"Come here, Solie."

Her brain said, "no wanna" but she forced her feet to move anyway. When she was just a few inches away, he motioned to his lap and simply said, "Sit."

She sat stiffly on one of his knees, her gaze focused on the table full of toys that she wasn't sure she could enjoy tonight. God, but she wanted to. She really did.

Arms wrapped around her, he pulled her back against his chest and nuzzled the top of her head as he spoke.

"This isn't about sex, Sols. It's about you. Understand?"

She nodded.

He smacked her lightly on her ass. "Words, Solie."

"Fine. Bossy ass…"

He smacked her again.

She yelped, "Yes. I understand."

"Good. Give me your wrist."

Without lifting her head, she held up one hand. Her thoughts scattered at what felt like a stiff leather cuff being tightened and secured. She shuddered.

She tried to remind herself why she was here, why she'd agreed to be his, to be with Burton.

I want this. I want him…

But you're not good enough. Even a sociopath didn't want you.

"Look at your wrists. Look at how the leather seems to fit just right." Words, quietly spoken. The breath warm against her forehead.

She glanced up and stilled.

They did fit just right…because they were hers. Mac must have slipped them to Burt when she wasn't looking. Boy, when those two conspired, they really went all out.

"I've seen you wear these on plenty of occasions. Watched from a distance as the white leather caressed that beautiful cinnamon skin. I always liked how the brown piping and trim matched your skin perfectly. The buckles used to catch the light whenever your arms were suspended. Beautiful."

But seeing the leather buckled in place again, surrounding her wrists made her feel…ill. Her brain tilted sideways at the memories that washed through her head, so fast if it had been a flood of water, she'd have drowned.

Thoughts of Marcais putting these same cuffs on her, telling her he loved her, calling her the perfect submissive…and then treating her as less than the dirt on the bottom of his combat boots. Not with the bondage, or the flogging or the spanking. But with his cheating, lying and subversion. The fucker.

"Now," Burton said, "I want you to take the cuffs off, and throw them in the trash over there." He pointed to a little wastebasket near the entrance to the space that she hadn't noticed before.

"Throw them away? But…why?"

"Do it. I'll tell you after."

A mix of anger and sadness had her biting back some choice expletives, not to mention a few tears.

When she was done, she turned to find Burton next to the table, waiting.

She didn't have to be told to go to him. She was far

from stupid…well, on most days.

Standing in front of him, Solie pictured a corner and the wall again. Why? Because she knew the man saw more than she wanted him to.

He held out a hand. She wanted to hide rather than put hers in it, but from somewhere inside she made that arm stretch out to her new man, and stay there.

Without a word, Burton put new cuffs around her wrists and tightened them just to the point of discomfort. The leather was unmarred. No tension marks or "broken in" areas. They were flawless, and surprisingly, matched the outfit she'd been wearing—red leather with black trim and bronze buckles.

He passed some red rope through the D-rings until her hands were loosely bound, and then led her over to one of the hooks secured to the wall. Burton pointed to one of the hooks that reminded her of something she'd hang a set of keys or a picture on—easy on, easy off.

"Loop the rope over the hook and face me."

Wait, what? He wasn't going to tie or secure her to anything? Didn't he think she could handle it, goddamn it?

"I had you throw away the other cuffs because they represented your old relationship, that guy's claim on your heart. His influence on your thoughts, feelings and emotions. I asked you to toss them, Sols, but bottom line is that you had to *choose* to do it. Just like you have to choose to accept these new cuffs from me. It's not a collar, but you will wear them when we're together."

Hmmm. Not quite what she had in mind, but Solie didn't say anything. Just glared at him, hating the memories the old cuffs had dredged up, and waited to see where this would go.

"Tell me how you felt when I put the old cuffs on you."

No. Couldn't form the words. Couldn't get them past

the lump in her throat. Tears she'd effortlessly kept in check came spilling down her cheeks.

Burton didn't comfort her. Simply stood and waited for her to get herself under control. It was the greatest gift he could have given her. It meant that he believed she was strong enough to get her shit together enough to have a conversation about this very painful subject.

After a few moments, she cleared her throat.

"May I have some tissue, please?"

Burton fished around in her play bag and brought her tissue. Solie unhooked herself from the wall and reached for it.

"Did I give you permission to release the rope from the hook?"

Shit. Just that quickly she'd forgotten that in this space and anytime they were together in private, he was boss. Hell, she even had it in writing as part of their earlier negotiations.

Solie put her hands back over her head, hooked the rope on the little hook on the wall.

Burton gently cleaned up her face and even held the tissue to her nose.

"Blow."

No way. That was just nasty. This morning when she'd let the waterworks loose, she'd taken care of her own snot rockets, thank you very much.

Burton cocked his head sideways. "Blow," he repeated.

She shook her head.

"Yes, Solie."

Frowned and turned her head away with a simple, "Nu-uh."

"Alright." The man was completely calm, neither face nor words held any trace of anger. But when he calmly said, "Put your clothes on. We're done here," panic, sheer and unmistakable, filled her chest. The word, "No!" came out in a rush as her heart pounded up into her throat.

"Excuse me?"

"I mean, I'll let you clean my nose. I don't want to go home. Not yet. Please."

"Solie, you know me, right?"

"Yes."

"And what would my typical response be?"

His gaze lasered to hers. His expression was unwavering, with body language to match. He was not happy with her just now. But he was being incredibly patient as well.

"Your typical response would be, too bad. We'd be leaving. Right now."

"I will say this and I will only say it once. I am not a D.I.N.O."

"I know, Burt, I just…"

"Do not interrupt."

Fingers wrapped around the rope between the cuffs and she held on for dear life, thankful for the knots on the ends. Her gut screamed that this moment would make or break what she wanted with this man.

"I am your friend, Solie. Will always be. But when I tell you to do something and your response is 'No', there is no negotiation at that point. If we're in the middle of a scene, the scene is done. To me, refusing an order is the same as screaming a safe word. Understand?"

"Yes. I understand."

Without taking his eyes off of her, he called out and Mac ducked back into the room. From her periphery, she saw Mac tilt her head as she looked back and forth between herself and Burton, but Solie didn't dare take her eyes off of his.

Thankfully, the other woman sat without a word and Burton continued as if there'd been no interruption at all.

And this time when he put the tissue to her nose, no

matter how much it made her feel like she was five years old, she blew.

"Why didn't you want to blow your nose, Solie?"

"You're going to get mad at me."

No response. Just…quiet. God, she'd give her left kidney for a little bit of white noise just now. Finally, she sucked in a deep breath and forced the words out.

"Because Marcais would yell at me when I cried. Made me feel like shit. Even if he was the reason for the tears, he would scream 'Stop fucking crying' like I'd physically harmed him or like I was crying for the hell of it or something."

The silent tears of a few moments ago became a gut-wrenching bawl. And Burton wiped her nose again. And she kept her hands exactly where they were supposed to be though it took all her effort not to snatch that box of tissue from his hands and run for it.

"Solie, you don't have to be strong all the fucking time," he growled. "I'm your port of harbor, your safe place to let it all out, like I have been for all the years you've known me. Turn around and face the wall."

The moment she did, his hands were on the bare skin of her back. The touch quieted, but not quite comforted. Eased up and down along either side of her spine, careful not to touch her tickle spots. Fingers pressed deeply into tense muscle at her neck and shoulders.

When her skin felt warm and her muscles loose and languid, the first light strike fell. Solie gasped. She could tell by the weight and impact, that it was a warm up flogger. The wash of pleasure was twofold—one, it just fucking felt good and two, it was only going to get better as he took her on tonight's journey.

Her mind took a quick trip down memory lane of what she'd put on that table. The three floggers ranged from very light leather to heavy strips of rubber. Of the two crops, one was your typical stiff one with a thin shaft covered with leather. The other had an ornate end of thick, pink, heart shaped plastic with little studs on it. It reminded her of the back of the mats people put on the floor of their cars.

Her mind flipped back to the present by the next strike. The impact was thuddy rather than stingy, followed by a gentle caress of his free hand on her skin, along the same path of the blows.

The dam she'd erected to protect her heart after the Marcais disaster began to strain under the pressure of the waves of desire for Burton that rolled up against it.

Desire was stoked and fostered by Burton's knowing hand and the energy he brought. Tonight, she was going to take it slow. Tonight, she was going to ease her way back into this part of her life. Right?

"Control your breathing, Solie."

What? Why? This was cake, nothing hard or…

"It's too soon. You're already starting to float away and we haven't really gotten started yet," Burt said.

Taking stock of herself, she ignored him. There wasn't any pain, no reason for alarm. She heard someone talking off in the distance. Sounded like they said something about someone floating away. Well, good for them. As for herself, she liked the way this felt. She hadn't had anyone touch her like this, or put a flogger to her skin in so very, very long, and it was just so good, and…

Smack!

"Ouch!" she yelped.

Burton had changed up his strokes, broken the rhythm and the force of the blows to yank her back from the sub-space edge.

"Well that certainly worked," she grumbled, her head clearing of any residual fog as he turned her to face him.

She glanced over at the table. He'd only made it to the fourth toy and she was toast. Damn.

"I want you to hear what I'm saying, Solie. Tell me you hear me."

It took a couple of tries, but she finally said, "I hear you. Loud and clear."

"Solie Shaw, you are the most desirable, together female I've ever met. You're loving, caring, giving."

Then his fingers were around her throat. Tightened just enough to make her aware of their presence, then a little bit more until she was keenly aware of exactly how much breath she was being allowed.

"You take care of your friends better than you take care of yourself." He lowered his head for a passion-filled kiss that set her body on fire. The weight of his hand against her skin, the total control he had over her as he collared her neck with his fingers, made her feel safe, secure and sexy in a way that nothing else did.

"You have your shit together and don't you dare allow the memory of some asshat to make you feel less than the spectacular woman you are."

He nipped her tongue and then her bottom lip as he deepened the contact. Held her tight so that his chest pressed against hers, his silk against her bare skin. Rubbed back and forth until her nipples pebbled and ached. Breath soughed in and out of her lungs.

The palm of his free hand skated over a bare breast. Up, down. Back and forth. Then a tug and a gentle pull with thumb and forefinger.

"Does that feel good?" he asked.

He knew it did, but one of the rules was that she must always answer a question, even if she thought it was stupid. So she gasped out, "Yes."

Then he tugged hard, harder, until the nipple throbbed and stung. The he stepped back just a bit to reach for something.

A second later, a riding crop tapped the tender skin of her breast. One, then the other, and back again. Over and over.

She squeezed her thighs together. Shifted up on her toes and back down, trying not to tug on the barely-there hook that her rope was laid over.

"Still good?"

"Oh god, yes. So good," she babbled, unable to quite catch her breath as the hand around her neck forced her head to the right.

Then he bit her.

"Ah god!"

Her determination to take it slow tonight slid down the river of her sensual desire. The moment the thick clear-pink heart with the little spiky things landed on the side of her ass cheek, her determination went clear out of sight.

She cried out.

"Sssh. Breathe through it, baby. You can do it." Burton's voice with just the right mix of encouragement and bossiness. The heart landed again, and again. She was sure to have bruises. The thought made her smile.

She would call that particular toy, "Brunhilda" from now on because it was one tough bitch.

Another blow. Burton wedged his knee between her thighs so that it rubbed against her clit.

It was over.

The wall around her vulnerability failed all together; and her emotions, infused with her true and natural sexuality, overflowed the banks of her need.

And she let it. Let it go. Let it take the path that it wanted to.

Until all she knew was the sensation of her man's hands around her neck, teasing and tormenting her breasts, skating over her stomach and her panty-clad ass. Brunhilda's sting on her glutes, her thighs. Burton's lips on her skin—sucking, nipping and biting.

Until knees began to buckle and...

"Please. Oh please, Burt," she begged.

Burt lifted the rope from the little keychain hook thingy, picked her up and eased down into the oversized chair with her in his lap again.

Suddenly a blanket was over them as Burt rocked her back and forth.

A thought poofed into her head—Burt with others. Flickers of his landing a flogger or a whip across someone else's skin. She'd even watched him create a butterfly pattern out of color-tipped needles on a woman's back before.

But Solie had never seen him give anyone aftercare when a scene was over. No one.

Yet that's exactly what he was doing with her. Using his hands to soothe, wrapping the blanket over her skin so she wouldn't get chilled. Holding a piece of chocolate to her mouth, encouraging her to eat it. Telling her how well she'd done after such a long time out of the scene. Even massaging her scalp a bit as she fell backward into the endorphin-laced waters of her mind.

CHAPTER FIVE

It had been a hell of a week, but all her deadlines were met for her current clients, she'd picked up a new contract, and had even sent off a congratulatory email to the consultants in Japan who'd landed the new business.

All hail geeks, because without people like Solie, the world just didn't turn. And that meant a nice living for her and her employees.

A glance out the window revealed an uncharacteristically clear day for the Pacific Northwest in early summer. Sunlight sparkled off the Sound and there wasn't a bit of fog to be seen.

She wasn't responsible for the weather, but that fact didn't keep a happy sigh from slipping past her lips as she linked her fingers behind her head, leaned back in her chair and actually put her feet up on her desk.

Yes, I fucking rock.

Add to that, she had a new-but-old fantabulous guy who'd given her space when she needed it, and hung around when she needed that, too. Burton had slept over this week and they'd began to develop a feel for each other.

Solie now automatically slipped on her new cuffs—which she loved, by the way—the moment he walked in the door. She'd learned that he liked to be greeted with a deep, passion filled kiss rather than a "hello" or a "how was your day".

And he'd learned that while she could plan the hell out of a business trip-for-two, she was never going to be the domestic type. Good thing she had sense enough to have a housekeeper or she'd be up to her neck in at least a year's worth of laundry.

She loved sharing her space with Burton. After she bought this place, Mac had designed her a Japanese bath, and Burton's company had built it. Glass brick walls and shoji screens made the space bright and airy. Tiled floors and big windows kept it comfortably cool even when steam filled up the room.

Each evening after a dinner that thankfully neither she nor Burton had prepared, they'd soaked in her Jacuzzi tub until they were limp noodles and relaxed from the stress of their day. Then Burton had let her wash him from stem to stern, which was a delicious journey all on its own.

Skin heated as she thought of how she'd oiled and massaged all that golden, tanned mountain of a man. Burton had muscles on top of muscles, or at least that's what it felt like under her fingers.

She'd sat, perched on his ass, worked coconut oil into the sculpted planes of his back, and along his ribs—he was ticklish, too—and down his hamstrings. Solie had paid special attention to his feet knowing that some days he spent a good deal of his day on them.

By the time she'd worked her way around to his front and down his thighs, his cock had been waving at her. God, she'd practically salivated with the desire to taste him. His natural scent mixed with the coconut oil had been like inhaling a pina colada. He just smelled so…juicy.

He's not even here and my mouth is watering right now. Gah!

Her reward for a job well done? Spankings. Lots and lots of spankings, followed by spooning until she'd fallen asleep. Burton knew she was two kinds of whores—a total shoe whore and a spanking whore. And this man delivered in both those areas.

What she really loved was that the man wasn't interested in turning her into someone she wasn't. He was interested in having her submission from her heart, not some contrived fake version of herself. And that rocked because that *other* guy…

Aw who cared about that other guy?

She now spent her time with Mr. Tall, Dark, and Domly. The up-close experience revealed exactly what kind of mojo he was packing. And Burton brought more to the table than she'd ever imagined.

She thought back on his words at Twilight Teahouse when he'd noticed her shoes and matching outfit. *"Damn, those sexy shoes are meant to be airborne."*

Solie had smiled then. And couldn't help but smile now.

She bounced out of her chair, happy with both her professional and personal lives. This called for dancing, which meant a flail of arms and legs around her office in some semblance of the Running Man. Her body felt light and her spirit even lighter. Add the growing heat in her flesh as a result of Burton's, uh, special focus on her. Damn near every night. All week long.

And, to top off her wonderful week, Solie had quietly made a visit to her doctor to make sure that her seven days of no sex were truly up. And yes, as of yesterday afternoon, sex with Burton was a-okay. After all the delicious attention he'd showered on her all week, she really, *really* wanted to share the ultimate intimacy with this man.

So now, it was Friday. Time to play.

But first, Solie logged onto Kinkfest.com, something she hadn't done since the last time she'd peeked at a certain someone's profile and ended up taking her battered heart from bruised to bloody, as well as getting her ass warmed in public.

Today she noticed a particular note on the "Today's Favorites" page. The person who wrote the post asked, "Why do some people feel the need to test your affection, push you away just to see if you come back? Perform destructive actions repeatedly to hurt themselves and the bond they have with you? Is it that they don't feel they deserve to be happy? That if they have a good, fulfilling and happy relationship that there is something dark hidden? To those people, I say that if you're trying to sink the boat, have the basic decency to let others out of the boat first before you go down with it like some poor suffering martyred soul."

Solie understood exactly where this woman was coming from. But unlike this female, Solie didn't need to ask this question—she already had the answer. The time she'd spent over the last few weeks with both herself and her friends had helped blow out the fog of post-breakup pain-n-rage brain. Today, she was centered, clear headed. Perhaps even half-way in control of her life.

Solie re-read the woman's post and smiled. Burt was right—Solie loved to be of service if she could. So she focused on her inner self, considered the woman's questions, and then poured her heart into an answer.

She wrote, "I read your post and I hope what I have to say is helpful without sounding preachy. I recently went through something similar, and here's what I truly believe—some people are just plain old broken. Common sense doesn't apply because they don't understand themselves. They are walking, damaged, abused, drama creators who are convinced it's everyone's fault but their own.

"It's Kinkfest.com's fault. It's Facebook's fault. It's their mama's fault. Their ex's fault. It's the UPS guy's fault. The weather man's fault. When it comes to the pain they cause others, you could stand before them bleeding from a hundred cuts yet they will swear it wasn't them who did the cutting; even though they're holding the sword with your blood dripping from it.

"Some are narcissists. Some are sociopaths. Some are cyberpaths. Some are psychopaths. Some are just plain predators who specialize in sabotaging themselves and you. They cultivate uncertainty and are good at keeping you off-balance by sowing seeds of doubt. Next thing you know, you begin to second guess yourself in areas where you'd always been confident. And a place like Kinkfest.com is attractive to those types. They are, in various forms, psychological, emotional, even financial and physical predators.

"For a large portion of the population, there is no explanation for why these people "poke you with a stick" other than the most common reason—dysfunction. The end.

"Is this everyone? Nope. Not at all. But I do believe, after having contact with these types, that it is a plausible answer to your question. Learn the signs and if you find yourself ready to commit, run instead. And if you're already in the boat, jump overboard and swim for shore."

A quick check for typos and Solie hit the send button.

Amazing, the lift a few shared words could do for a person—and not the one receiving, but the one giving. With a spring in her step and a dash of pep in her attitude, Solie left the computer exactly as it was, grabbed the house keys off the hook, patted her shepherd on the head and headed out the door.

A broad grin spread across her lips even as the pack of drunk butterflies dive bombed her gut because Burton stood on the front porch.

How the hell a man could make leaning against a deck railing look sexy, she would never know. Her moment of surprise morphed into giddy expectation…and giddy was not a word she associated with herself. Ever.

But Burton just seemed to bring the "little" out in her sometimes.

She didn't bother asking why he'd come here instead of meeting her at the local patisserie for lunch. Whatever his reasons, she didn't really care. Solie just stood there and took him in for a moment. Yep, the man standing on her porch looked good enough to *be* her lunch rather than the soup and sandwich she'd planned to order shortly.

She still felt the impact of those mesmerizing blue eyes, even when hidden behind dark shades. God, he just hummed with a crazy vibrancy that made the skin on her arms erupt in goose bumps. Arms crossed a wide chest that was tastefully covered in his favorite, royal purple silk. He must be off work today. No pressed slacks or suit. Instead he sported a pair of jeans that fit so perfectly she wondered if they were tailored.

Her next thought was curiosity as to where he preferred to have his things cleaned. Solie pulled back from that thought. She and Burton had already negotiated that point—she would not be taking on any domestic tasks for him.

For now, it was all about her, and her emotional and physical needs. Period. And the stubborn ass man wouldn't be moved from that point no matter how much she insisted that she could handle more.

So as he waited for her to come down the steps she

was back to ogling the muscled forearms that peeked out from beneath the short sleeves. They were ropey and well-formed, sprinkled with the same dark hair that was on his head and...

"Keep looking at me like that, Sols, and we won't make it out of here."

"Uh, and that's bad?"

"Smart ass." Then he just stood and waited with that damn brow raised. Solie bit her lip to keep from smiling but it didn't really work. He grinned right back as she greeted him with the kiss he wanted, and the kiss she was beginning to love to give. Up on her toes, she simply said, "Hi", and then poured herself into a lip lock that she hoped curled his toes.

When his arms wrapped around her and lifted her against his body with a moan, she lit up inside knowing that the simple contact had him making that delicious sound.

Set back on her feet, Burton stepped back as his fingers trailed over the skin of her neck. He took off his shades and Solie gulped. Oh man, the look he laid on her as he backed away, walked around to the passenger side of his truck and opened the door for her stopped the breath in her lungs.

"Stop eyeballing me, woman, and move your ass."

After all, they were on a schedule and he still hadn't told her why he'd come to pick her up for lunch instead of meeting her at the eatery as planned. But the moment she got a good look at the sparkling mischief in his eyes, she was sure it would be an afternoon to remember.

* * * * *

"You're always in such control. You don't really have a choice, and I'm sorry for that. I know you long to relax, but you just don't have the time, or the chance...or a person who will *make* you."

He was right…but she didn't particularly feel like admitting it just now so she sat, put on her "Me no need nobody" face and sipped her cola in silence.

"Today, I'm that person, Solie."

He snatched her glass and slid his lemon water over to her side of the table. Head tilted a hard left as she started to open her mouth.

"Unless this is your diabetic cheat day, you'll have lemon water with your food. Period."

Fuck. And she really wanted that cola, more for the kick than anything else. After all, her successful week came with the sacrifice of a nice chunk of sleep. Even if the man across the table was responsible for some of those lost zzzz's and late nights, if Solie was honest with herself—which she made a habit of doing—she needed neither the sugar nor the caffeine.

Burt sat back, all long legs, wide buffed chest and healthy tanned skin. So tall, it looked like someone had folded him into that chair. Add piercing blue eyes against the backdrop of jet black stylish hair, and he looked so delicious, she wanted to just gobble him up and skip lunch all together.

God, it was nice to look at a man and not have to fight that sick sinking feeling of betrayal in her gut, or that anxious knot lodged in her throat almost cutting off her air.

Taking in Burton Khrys was an exercise in decadence, plain and simple.

"Now, where were we? Oh yes, today I'm going to get you to think on nothing but us and what we're doing together. No work. No clients."

He'd reached across the table again, but this time work roughened fingers massaged her palm as he held her gaze. The words were smooth as silk, quietly spoken so only she heard, but her gut did a freefall at the underlying steel of his tone. And suddenly, all of the need to display her everyday bad-assness just…melted away. It felt wonderful.

"What I'm going to tell you to do will push the boundaries of our friendship and our new relationship. Do you trust me?"

For a second her brain got stuck on the words "tell you to do".

Burton Khrys? Alpha boss to her alpha bitch. A different animal. Primal. Earthy. He seriously flipped her subby switch. So instead of calling him on his "tells" rather than "asks", Solie answered his question.

"Yes, I trust you."

"Do you believe that I'd never do anything to harm you?"

She took a sip of lemon water. It was actually pretty refreshing. Good call on his part. Another swallow, then she said, "Burt, I trust you and I agree to whatever it is you're going to ask me to do." She'd deliberately said *ask* instead of *tell* and then bit back a smile when he gave her the raised eyebrow and stern look. "You don't have to keep asking me that. I meant it when I answered you the first time."

"You giving me attitude, Sols?"

"Nope. I'm just sayin'." Besides, every woman had to push her boundaries every now and again. His fingers still stroked her palm, stoking a fire low in her belly that trickled clear down to her toes.

"Do we need to negotiate, woman?"

"Nope. Bring it."

Oh, she was really feeling her Wheaties just now, but she knew she wouldn't regret it. From the stern set of his jaw, it appeared that nice Burton—*oxymoron*—was gone and Mr. Thuddy Paddle-hands was in attendance. Actually, now that she thought about, he was always present. Just not always quite so…

"Well all-righty then." He handed her a little black plastic bag. "Here you go. Off to the bathroom. You'll know what to do with it. See you when you get back."

The bathroom? Oh my goodness.

She rose on wobbly legs with a feeling of both excitement and impending doom. She must be crazy because the thought made her smile inside. When she opened the bag in the ladies room, boy was she glad she'd worn a pair of regular panties instead of a sexy thong or something.

Back at the table, Solie sat gingerly and stared at the man across the table from her. Her yoga pants felt a bit more snug just now.

"Give me the remote." She wasn't stupid enough to mistake it for anything other than what it was—an order.

She handed it over, and watched closely as he fiddled with it in his lap, and then gave it right back to her.

"Turn it on."

"But there are no batteries in it. I already che…" She flipped the switch and went still as the toy she'd inserted into her pussy fired up and her nerve endings went full tilt.

So that's what he was doing. Putting batteries in the thing.

"Turn it half way up and let's go get our food."

Then he winked and left her sitting there?

Was he nucking futs? Go get food? They were at a Mongolian grill where she had to serve up her own veggies and meat, and then take it to the cook to grill it. How was she supposed to do that with a vibrator humming away in her pants?

And Burton was over at the buffet filling his bowl. She sat and stared. The man didn't even turn and look to see if she was coming.

Oh, you'll be coming, all right.

Damn it, she could do this…quaking knees and all.

Maybe it was her ego talking, but who knew? She wanted to pass this little test for two reasons—she wanted to prove she could keep her shit together while being totally distracted, and she wanted to please her guy.

Solie sucked in a breath, rose from her seat, ever grateful she'd worn tennis shoes today, and hustled on over to the buffet.

Just keep breathing, just keep breathing. You know, like the blue fish in that Nemo movie. Just keep swimming, just keep swimming.

By the time she made it back to her seat, her palms were sweaty and her hands were shaking about as fast as the little silver bullet stuffed up her pussy.

Burt sat down, turned somewhat sideways in his chair and crossed his legs. Chopsticks in hand, he began to tuck in. "Turn it all the way up. Now talk to me."

Talk to him? Hell she could barely eat her...whatever it was she had in her bowl. Damn chopsticks hit the tabletop three times before he took mercy on her and handed her a fork.

God, it felt like she had a sign propped on top of her head that said, "I have a vibrator stuffed up my hoo-haa. It's flipped to *high* and I want to come SO bad!" On the other hand, she also wanted to kick Burton under the table for coming up with the idea, and then run for it. Maybe that would wipe the shit-eating grin off of his face...but somehow she doubted it.

"Are you close to coming, Solie?" he asked, then popped a piece of grilled shrimp into his mouth. She wondered if it was delicious considering everything she had on her plate tasted the same—like out-of-reach-orgasm, if she had to give the flavor a name.

Sitting back in her chair, Solie pushed away the food she'd been picking over, and gave up fighting the sensations coursing through her body.

She could feel the hum everywhere. Her inner thighs quivered, ass cheeks clenched, knees locked tight. Toes were prepared to curl inside her tennis shoes. Because an orgasm was coming. And it wasn't sneaking up on her. No, it was chasing her, barreling down on her like a cargo train.

Burt had said something. Had asked her a question.

Her brain ran to catch up to the rest of her body. It was losing the race. Badly.

"Solie, no coming without permission," he whispered.

"Huh?" She knew her eyes had begun to droop to half-mast. Didn't care. At all.

"Solie?" He reached under the table, grabbed her knee and squeezed hard.

She jerked in her seat, but it wasn't quite enough to bring her around. So he did it again.

Three times must be the charm because finally she raised her gaze to meet his. Even her eyes felt…wobbly.

"Baby, you look absolutely adorable and goofy."

Well that was enough to pull her completely back from the brink.

Goofy? As if.

Burton laughed out loud.

Solie glanced around. Burton's laugh had caught the attention of a few diners. In fact, several women watched him as he watched Solie.

A swift wind of anxiety kicked up and blew away a bit more of the fog in her horny brain. And just as quickly, she pushed back and chose to sink into the cocoon of need that Burton weaved around her with his words and wicked grin.

After all, he wasn't looking at those women, or returning their attention. This was her best friend, and he'd never been a cheater. He'd pledged himself to *her* a week ago. Had given *her* his unwavering friendship years ago. His toy hummed inside of *her*. And when they left, he'd be going with *her*.

"Any plans for this afternoon, Sols?" he asked, chugging the last of his, uh, her cola.

She shook her head. "Took the rest of the day off."

"Good. Leave your plate. By the time we get to TT, you're going to beg me to come."

TT? He was taking her to Twilight Teahouse in the middle of the day? Well, they did have a light luncheon tea and menu. But they'd just eaten. Was he taking her to the upper floors? She knew they were available for play at this hour, but she'd just never taken the time to go up to Seattle at mid-day. The traffic alone was a total buzz kill.

Would she have to sit through an agonizingly long bumper-to-bumper ride with a buzzing toy stuffed up her cooch? This gave a whole new meaning to the term "crotch rocket".

Oh god, Solie wasn't sure she could take it.

Burton was on his feet staring at her with a receipt in his hand. When had he paid the bill? Holy hell, she really was drifting in and out of it, whatever "it" was. Just now she had no words.

She grasped the hand extended to her.

"Come along, my googly-eyed beauty."

She snorted, but didn't even bother trying to talk. Googly eyed? Pffft.

Her head said, "Fuck you." But there was no denying that her body said, "Fuck me!"

CHAPTER SIX

Solie handed over the remote when asked, then buckled herself in. She barely noticed the movement of the truck as they sped along, unless Burton hit a bump in the road. Those, she felt profoundly.

God, her fingers trembled. Legs were restless. Skin felt stretched too tight. Pussy was on fire.

Not being allowed to come was exquisite torture. The entire ride from their lunch spot to downtown Seattle, Solie experienced longing, rage and every emotion in between, courtesy of Burton and that fucking remote control.

Every time she thought her mind was about to completely slip, Burton upped the ante.

"A little added sensation, beautiful," he drawled right before a thick fist delivered a thuddy blow to the thickest part of her thigh muscle. The impact of his hand combined with the sizzle of the nerve endings from the sensual sensation was, God, just delightful.

She was going to come. Just couldn't help it.

Right before detonation, Burton dialed the vibrator down to the lowest setting and all the movement in her channel came to a halt.

"Fuck!" She screamed. Yelled. Practically sobbed. Then he was slapping her thigh again, a lovely and calculated combination of thuddy and stingy blows.

"I've been counting the days, Solie. My dick is about to burst thinking about that sweet pussy. Waking up to the scent of your arousal and not being able to have you has been killing me. So I want to drive you absolutely crazy. Promise I'll join you there shortly after."

He steered his beast-of-a-truck with one hand, and the other was buried in her locs.

"I love your hair. I love that I can pull on your dreads, yank them the way you like, and you won't scream about how I mess up your hair-do." Now his fingers drew circles on her scalp. Round and round. Up and down. Soft strokes followed by the easy *scratch, scratch, scratch* of short blunt nails.

And then he pulled.

Solie slammed her eyes shut, squeezed her thighs together and bit down on her lip to keep from yelling out her pleasure. He hadn't told her to keep quiet. There was just a bit of stubborn in her that was still trying to hold it together.

Finally, she gasped, "Oh God, please!"

"Almost there, baby. Just hold on. Almost there, I promise." Burt's words were barely a whisper, yet the impact could be felt from eyebrows to baby toes.

And she wasn't the only one in sorry shape. Her man wasn't immune to what he was doing to her. The evidence was in the barely-there hitch of his breath when she'd screamed. The dampness on his palm as he ran his free hand up and down her forearm.

Knowing that his desire was being pushed and pummeled by hers only sent her trip higher.

Crazy? Yes, that pretty much summed up where she was right now. She was in Loonyville. Tooty in the head. Brimming with bonkers. Coo-coo for Cocoa Puffs.

By the time they pulled into the underground parking garage at Twilight Teahouse, Solie was damn near ready to pass out.

Burton walked around to the passenger side and opened her door. Could her legs even support her weight? The better question was, did she care? Burton was big enough, and certainly strong enough to carry her without any problem so she decided to let him.

He switched the vibrator back on for a split second, then turned it off again.

Solie went still. Held her breath and waited to see if he would change his mind. Again. The last thing she needed was to think she was in the clear, step out of the car and then fall flat on her face when the sensation kicked back in.

Hey, she'd made a rhyme. Such a talented lady at multi-tasking.

Oh wait. Not a rhyme. Just her brain cells imploding.

She laughed, cackled actually.

"Need a second?" Burt asked as she swung her legs around so she could hop out of the vehicle.

A second passed. Then two. Solie made no move to actually get out.

Burt grinned. "I'd offer to carry you, but even in your current sorry state—"

"Sorry?" she hissed. "You put me in this state, by the way."

"—I still don't think you'd let me carry you anywhere."

Well he had that right. It didn't matter that she'd just told herself that she'd let him toss her over his shoulder if he wanted. Now that he'd pushed her particular "independent woman" button, she would walk on her own two feet until the moment that she couldn't stand up any longer. And based on the experience so far, she just might reach that point pretty soon.

She looked around the parking lot that was for private club members only. No public parking to be had—not even for those who came to enjoy the unique and delicious fare in Twilight Teahouse.

"Quite a few more cars here than I'd expect for a mid-day romp. What are we doing here, Burton?"

"Don't worry. I wouldn't invite anyone into our play unless we'd discussed it. And honestly I'm not anxious to share you at all. As for today, you've done so well denying yourself multiple orgasms, I think you deserve a treat."

She eyeballed him but didn't ask what kind of treat. Besides, he knew full well that she was curious, and if he wanted to tell her, then he would.

"I asked Kuri to hold a play room for us, just in case we made it out here today. Fourth floor. Japanese baths."

An unfamiliar sound erupted out of Solie's throat. It kind of sounded like a...squeal. Solie was sure she'd never made that sound before, but immediately didn't care. Out of the car, not only were her legs steady, she practically ran Burton over trying to get to the elevator.

Solie and Mac took advantage of the spa on the second floor at least once a month. Nothing kinky, just a slice of mani-pedi heaven. However, the fourth floor was couples only—no exceptions. She'd wanted to experience the Japanese themed play space forever, but the ex-dude hadn't been interested. Solie learned later that one of the many women he'd slept around with worked up there—big surprise. Not!

And now, thanks to Mr. Burton Khrys, here she was at last.

This man is racking up some serious lucky points.

Once inside the sleek elevator, Solie pushed the button for the fourth floor. Doors slid closed but the elevator didn't move.

Shit.

She didn't have her little magnetized access keycard to the club.

Damn it, damn it, damn it.

Burton reached past her, swiped his keycard and Solie let out a sigh of relief.

Though her sex was heated and throbbing, her underwear was soaked and the damn things were beginning to cool against her skin, the only words in her head were "clothes", "off" and "now".

Relief. She needed it badly. But more than that, Solie needed Burton, the man, not just what he could give her, or do for her. She needed his special kind of tenderness. His own unique brand of care.

Suddenly he was there, pressed against her even as her back was flush against the cool frosted glass of the elevator wall. She drank from his lips as if his kiss were her oasis in the dessert. He'd been raining life on her own particular parched heart for years. She just hadn't realized the depth of it until now. All the love and care he'd shown in their platonic relationship was just as solid and sincere now that they'd decided on an intimate pairing.

And now that she'd had a taste, Solie loved kissing Burt. The man put all his emotion and intention into every kiss, every time.

He'd told her when he'd picked her up for lunch today that she would focus on nothing but the two of them. No work. No clients. The man had been so right—her concentration was on him, *them*. No one and nothing else. Not her past. Nor her future. Hell, not even the present, with the exception of where this elevator was headed.

Burton broke the kiss, but Solie kept her eyes closed and waited to see, *feel*, what was next.

Her man flipped her around, grabbed her by the hair

and pulled her head sideways. Then he bit her on *that* spot—the one that made her unsteady and her entire body quiver. He bit her again, then sucked the skin just there. Solie's knees buckled. Burton caught her and lifted her into his strong, brawny arms with no effort. Barely a moment later, the elevator dinged.

God help her, they'd reached the fourth floor already?

Doors slid open and she felt Burton move. Head buried in his chest, she listened to the solid thump of a strong heart, heard him speak briefly to someone, and then they were off again.

A traditional Japanese bath meant scrubbing down in the shower, and then soaking in a deep tub for relaxation. Images floated through her head of Burton's lean and muscular body as she'd washed him in her own bath at home. All that deeply tanned skin, sprinkled with dark hair on ropey defined arms. The sculpted chest slick with ginger soap as she played with the single nipple ring that graced his left pectoral. Solie almost smiled against his shirt just now as she remembered how the thick beautiful cock had tapped her forehead as she'd scrubbed his quads thoroughly. His groans of pleasure as her fingers glided over his perfect ass.

Women would kill for an ass like Burton Khrys. Just...*dayum.*

"Thank you," Burt said with a hearty laugh.

"Huh?"

"You complimented my ass. Glad you like it."

"Wait, what? Oh, never mind. You must be the only man on Earth that makes me say things out loud when I don't mean to." Solie tried to sound grumpy, she really did. But his fingers were teasing the underside of her breast and she tried to bury her face even deeper into his chest as he hurried along.

"Like I said earlier, adorably goofy."

Smart ass.

"Really?" Burt snorted. "I think you've just earned yourself a spanking with your orgasms."

Yep. I'm definitely gone in the brain.

Only she made sure to keep that particular thought to herself.

* * * * *

Solie found herself carried into an immaculate cream and lapis blue shower that was big enough for at least ten people. A little wooden stool sat in the middle of the space.

Just as Burton set her on her feet an attendant came in.

"I'll see you in the soaking tub shortly, okay Solie?"

She must have looked disappointed because then he said, "I told you this was a treat for you. Not service for me. Not right now. Enjoy your shower and the attendant will bring you to me. Oh, and the bathroom is over there. Go and take care of things, but no touching yourself. That's all mine."

He gave her a quick kiss, and left. After a trip to the bathroom, the evil bullet vibrator was washed and tucked away in her clothing. The attendant already had the water at the perfect temperature when she came out of the restroom. The woman washed her with sugar scrub until she was sure her skin glowed.

Ten minutes later, her entire body felt as solid as a wet noodle as she was led to the soaking room.

Her breath lodged in her throat as she caught sight of her man standing there waiting for her. He wore a traditional blue robe and stood next to a bank of windows that looked out over the city. She caught the glint of sun off the deep blue water of the Sound and swore it was close enough to dive into from here.

The tub was huge, more like a big sunken pool rather than a soaking tub. Burt motioned her into the water, shed his robe and stepped down onto the first step. He wore not a stitch. And that was just the way Solie liked him.

"Come over here, Solie."

She eased into the pool with a sigh. The temperature was perfect—not too hot, not too cool. Solie waded over to him and sat down in a spot that caused the water to level out just below her breasts.

"No, right here."

He pointed to his lap and the dusky pole of a cock that was almost purple at the head.

Oh my goodness. She'd been turned on high for a good part of the day and even though the shower attendant washed her with not a single indication of horniness, Solie was still on a medium simmer.

If she sat on his lap she wouldn't last long.

Wait a minute, what in the world was she thinking? Who said she had to last at all? This man wasn't going to play games with her. He wasn't going to offer her a lollipop and then snatch it away when she reached for it.

No. That was another life. One that didn't deserve her emotional attention.

This was her and Burton's time, and that's where she would keep her thoughts. Period.

So she eased over to him and sat on his lap. With a gasp, she found herself face down over this lovely thighs, with his cock pressing into her stomach.

"First, let's get this out of the way, courtesy of your favorite smart ass."

His palm landed on her ass with a loud *schwack*. Holy fuck! Her skin was wet from both the shower and the quick trip across the tub, and it caused the mother of all stings when his hand connected with the damp flesh.

By the third whack Solie was ready to float away.

Four.

Five.

She was moaning, gasping his name.

Six.

Seven.

Begging was imminent.

Eight.

Nine.

Ten.

"Oh please. Please, Burton…"

She was so boneless her legs just fell open as she panted in an attempt to catch her breath.

"Mmm, look at that. That pussy is so wet and pretty. You're ready aren't you?"

A nod was all she could manage as all the stimulation of the day swirled together and crashed down over her libido like a thunderstorm that had been building in the summer heat.

Just before thick fingers slid into her swelling folds, he stopped. "I'm going to do a wet check, all right?"

"Yes," she breathed.

And then he was stroking her, slipping the pad of his index finger against the resisting ring of muscle at her entrance. The other hand explored the blushing skin of her ass. Solie found herself quickly moving past want into pure, unmistakable need.

With each dip, her hips wound in a larger and larger circle until she was practically humping his hands.

It didn't matter that the silken heat of his cock scalded the skin of her stomach. It didn't matter that he obviously wanted her as much as she wanted him. Burton wouldn't give her what she craved until she asked for it. Nicely.

"P…Please fuck me. Please."

"And why should I do that, Solie?"

"Because I need it."

"And why else?" He pressed two fingers deep into her sex. She almost came on the spot.

"Because I deserve it."

"Deserve what?"

She knew what he was after. It was a conversation that they'd had on more than one occasion throughout their friendship. And Solie knew it to be true, so she didn't hesitate.

"I deserve to be loved without conditions. I deserve to be treated like the queen that I am. I deserve to have what I desire. And in a D/s dynamic, I deserve to be rewarded when I have earned it."

"Good girl. And today, you have definitely earned a reward. You were amazing, kept your sanity long beyond what I expected. And you didn't come. Not once. So let's fix that."

Without another word, Solie found herself in the tub with her chest flat against the cool tiles where Burton had been sitting only moment before.

With an ass cheek in each hand, the man spread her wide, then worked himself inside until he was slick with her juices. Then he was *there*, the entire length of him stretched and filled her, until she swore that if she were looking in a mirror she'd see his cock reflected in her eyes.

One hand buried in her hair and the other stroking every inch of flesh he could reach. And it was so good. Each stroke was better than the last, better than every dream she'd ever had about this man. Better than a new pair of sexy strappy high heeled shoes!

And then she was coming, and coming and coming. Making up for each orgasm she'd denied herself earlier. And when she thought she was all wrung out, Burton proved her wrong twice more.

By the time he found his own pleasure deep inside her pussy, Solie was damn near cross eyed and beyond noddle-boned.

It was the best lunch-date-turned-dinner-date EVAH!

* * * * *

Later on that night, Solie woke abruptly. She rolled over and took in the sight of the man next to her. She seldom used the fireplace in her bedroom, but the sunny day had turned into a fog-filled chilly night. The embers glowed just enough to cast the most beautiful light on her best friend.

And grabbed her journal, flipped on a small reading light so as not to wake Burt, and she began to write.

Eight weeks ago she'd been beyond heartbroken, the pain so tangible that when she looked in the mirror it seemed etched into her very skin.

Eight weeks ago, a confidence that had never been in question before had teetered on the ledge of her surety. Why? Because the person that was supposed to love her, treasure her, care for and keep her, had been on the wrong side of everything.

He'd spoken to and about her in a manner that was far beyond unkind.

Had yelled and screamed at her, pushed into her space, gotten in her face. When she'd finally had enough and asked why he treated her in such a manner his response had been, "Because I can."

If she'd been honest, that was the day she knew it was over. Her heart had known what her mind didn't want to accept.

Eight weeks ago she'd learned that the man that had lived in her house, slept in her bed, spent time with her family and friends, had also done those same things with countless other women…all at the same time.

She'd given and given and given—her mind, body, soul, money, food, her trust and her time. All he had to do was ask for it, and it had been his.

It was in her nature to give. It was a part of herself that she couldn't simply turn off, and had no desire to, although at that time she'd wished otherwise, if only to keep some part of herself from being emotionally stomped into the carpet.

Eight weeks ago, she'd tallied up what he'd given her and it amounted to nothing more than a lovely spanking or two, a broken heart...and an STD.

But that was eight weeks ago. And this was now.

Was she still healing? Sure. But the hurt was barely there. The heartache almost completely healed until the cracks in her heart were now full of love for herself and the man whose arm was thrown over her waist. Gone was the fire-driven anger that had been a companion of sorts. Now, there was only pity and compassion for Marcais, a man who would never truly know love.

Solie was free. In every way that she needed to be, she was free.

And not so free.

She was in service to Burton Khrys, his companion and lover. And this bondage was a sort that she welcomed any day of the week.

With that, she tucked away her journal, clicked off the reading light and decided to dream of what she would look like in the new red and white bamboo and silk rope Burton had given her after he'd brought her home from a most wondrous and playful afternoon that faded seamlessly into an equally wondrous night.

CHAPTER SEVEN

In the early darkness of the morning, Burton woke her up with tender lovemaking that quickly morphed into the rough-and-tumble loving she craved.

After coming three times, they landed in a hot and deliciously sweaty heap with the sheets a tangle around their feet.

Out of the blue, a final remaining dam Solie hadn't been aware of, broke inside of her.

Burton gathered her into his arms and squeezed tight. "What's wrong, Solie? What is it?"

"Nothing is wrong. It's perfect actually. You've given me back to myself," she sobbed.

"No, darlin', you did that all on your own."

Her mouth dropped open when he eased her away from his body so he could look into her eyes. A solitary tear slid down his cheek. His words were solid without a single waver. If she hadn't been looking at him just now she wouldn't have believed it.

"Here's what Marcais didn't understand, Solie. A Dom isn't just someone that tells you to strip, bends you over the sofa or his knee and gives you forty whacks.

112

The man was obviously never taught to take care of his things. He didn't know the difference between rough sex and being a Dominant, baby. Anyone can Dom a doormat, just like anyone can tie up a woman and then tell her not to move. Me, I'd rather place your arm where I want it, tell you not to move and know that you can move—but won't.

Anyone can declaw a cat and then feel high and mighty because it can't scratch. But honestly, darlin', I'd rather have you just the way you are, claws and all, knowing that you keep them sheathed just for me.

God, I adore you. You're strong and I respect that. That guy's issue had to do with his character, not yours. I guess for some fucked up reason he felt that if he convinced you that you were 'less than', then it would make him feel 'more than'. Solie, you're an amazing woman. And the fact that you submit to me because you choose to makes me the luckiest bastard alive."

"Thank you, Burt. Thank you so much for that." Watery smile and all, she leaned up and kissed him. And Burt being Burt, she soon found herself underneath him moaning out her pleasure before slipping back into a peaceful sleep.

*　*　*　*　*

Something went from knocked out to fully awake in seconds. Her heart pumped furiously and a chill traveled up the back of her neck. She felt...watched. Like something or someone was in the room with her. Rather than rolling over and jerking herself out of bed to fight, she stretched, rolled over slowly and kept her eyes lashes lowered so that her eyes were mere slits.

Arms over her head, she peeked toward the door and then wrapped her arms around her pillow and snuggled in with what she hoped was a convincing sleepy sigh.

She lay there in the dim light of the new dawn and stilled as if she'd fallen back asleep.

And something was wrong. She knew it.

The dog had barked, but as quickly as she'd started up with her deep shepherd voice, loud enough to wake the dead, she'd stopped. Must have been a squirrel outside or something.

Then the bedroom door moved. Slowly. Deliberately. Until it closed with a quiet swish. Maybe it was Burt? Yes, that was it. It was Burt just checking in on her before he left to go get breakfast. No need to be worried, right?

When the tingle wouldn't go away, Solie forced herself to relax and drift back to sleep. Only, sleep wouldn't come, damn it.

After half an hour of pretending to snore with no further noise or door movement, she got up and hit the shower.

"May as well start the day," she grumbled.

Ten minutes and a protein shake later, with leash in hand she headed out to walk the dog.

If there were any farms nearby, she was sure she'd beat the chickens awake, it was so quiet out. The dew on the grass as she jogged began to seep into her shoes to make her socks damp. The fog was thick and the humidity felt good on her face. It was the only skin showing since she'd bundled up against the chilly Pacific Northwest July morning.

"Some summer we're having, right, Mims," she said to the dog. Then she laughed at herself. What a bundle of contradictions she was…well, sometimes.

"Damn. Time to go back Mims. Sorry, girl. I need to get my day moving."

Around the corner from her house, Solie ducked into the wide, clean alley that separated the townhouses down the street from her house. Almost to her back door, she slammed to a halt.

Marcais Dupree, nutball extraordinaire, stood there in the dim light of the dawn watching her.

"What the fuck are you doing here?" she snapped.

"What do you mean what the fuck am I doing here?"

"Why are you near my house?"

"I have a friend in this area. And what's it to you? I can go wherever the fuck I want to go whenever I feel like it."

With each word he walked closer, bowing up his chest at her, his words bitten off at the ends as if he wished he could chew her up and spit her out. His body language screamed violence and she hated that her muscles were tensed for fight or flight.

At one time, she would have never been afraid of this man.

But that was then and this was now.

Mims must have picked up her nervousness because she started to growl. The noise drew Marcais' attention, thankfully.

"Well, have a good day. Come on, Mims." And Solie walked on toward her house taking a wide berth around the man who stared daggers at her.

From behind his words punched her in the back.

"So you left me for that faggot, Burt, I see."

Left him for Burt? Was he out of his mind?

Oh yeah. Sociopath, remember? Duh.

"I didn't leave you for anyone, Marcais. You cheated. You lied. I walked. And I have it on good authority that you're carrying right on with one of your mistresses as if she was always your world rather than your secret. So fuck you. Now if you'll excuse me, I have a jog to finish and work to do."

With that, she forced her legs to jog rather than flee, pulled her key from her sweatpants pocket before she was even close to the door, and ducked inside at record speed.

Heart pumping, she knew that she'd just defused a time bomb. The expression on his face chilled the marrow in her bones. The anger. The malice. It didn't make any sense, given she'd been nothing but good to the man. The fact that he was angry because he thought she'd left him for Burt was more than unsettling given it had no place in reality whatsoever. It didn't even make any sense.

Wait a minute. How the hell did Marcais know she was seeing Burton? Having Burt at her house was no new thing, even when she'd still been with Marcais, Burt and Mac spent plenty of time over here. He'd been banned from the Twilight Teahouse after they got wind that he was passing cooties around so no one there would dare tell him her business. So how in the hell did he know what she was doing in the privacy of her own home?

Sociopath. She had to keep reminding herself. She slipped the leash off of the dog, toed off her damp sneakers and locked every door in the house.

Mac had used her considerable connections in the Army and learned that Marcais was being reassigned to Germany soon. Well, Germany couldn't get here fast enough, damn it. Yep. He was a time bomb all right—one that needed to completely go away so she didn't have to worry about it detonating anywhere near her.

* * * * *

Shortly after Solie had booted up her computer with the determination to concentrate on work, Burt showed up with coffee and Dunkin' Donuts. Work all but forgotten, she left her office, ducked into the bedroom to put on her leather cuffs and grab her meds, and then met her man in the living room.

Burt sat on the couch and Solie chose a spot on the floor between Burt's legs. She sunk her bare feet into the thick plush carpet with a sigh. "Ooh, I think I'm in love," she mumbled around a bit of carb-loaded perfection. "Timing is perfect." She took another bite and followed it down with a gulp of strong coffee. The stuff was so hot it burned all the way down her throat, but it tasted so good she didn't care.

As they ate, Solie told of how surprised she'd been when Marcais appeared like some vengeful spirit out of the fog.

"I don't like that he's hanging around here out of the blue, Solie. You know he's bat-shit crazy from his whacked out behavior with you. And if the stories his ex-wife told you are true, this man can be dangerous."

The doorbell rang. Solie jumped.

"Okay, I really don't like that you're wound up so tight, woman. At all." Burt got up off the couch and walked out of the living room. Mims joined him as he headed to the front door. A few moments later he called out, "Solie, come here, darlin'."

God, she loved when the country-boy came oozing out of his pores. Such a gentleman. Sort of.

At her man's side, Solie smiled at her neighbor from down the street.

"Hi, Miss Solie. Sorry to disturb you this early in the morning, especially on a Saturday, but I wanted to catch you before I head out to the base."

"No problem, Grange. What's up?"

"Well, my wife thinks it's nothing but I'm not so sure so I'm just gonna tell you. We've been seeing a black truck cruising up and down the neighborhood."

Her stomach hit the floor.

"And it seems to slow down near your house and then keeps going. And a couple of weeks ago I noticed someone coming in and out through your back door when you're not at home. And sometimes it's really late at night, like two and three in the morning.

My wife figured it was your boyfriend or something. But after comparing notes, we realized that it's not the same person." With that he nodded at Burt.

"So, what does this person look like?" Burt asked. Solie braced herself for the reply.

"Tall, about six foot three. Big. You know, muscular big, not fat big. Bald. Dark skin."

"Really?" she asked too brightly. "Well, thanks. I appreciate you looking out for me. But it's all good. No worries."

"Good. I was hoping everything was okay."

"So how long are you down range this time, Grange?"

"Just a quick tour and I'll be back in no time. It's my last deployment before I retire and neither my wife nor I can wait."

"I understand that, for sure. Let your sweetie know that if she needs some company while you're gone she's welcome to come over in her pj's and watch corny movies with me any time. I'll even provide the popcorn."

"Thanks, Solie. I appreciate that, ma'am. Take care."

The moment she closed the door, Burt wrapped her up in his arms and whispered, "I'm staying here today. You're not going to your office across town either. It's him, Solie. Coming in and out. Now we know why that key disappeared out of the spare key drawer."

And why the back door had been unlocked when she was sure she'd locked it. Hell, even Mac had caught it a time or two.

"But that key isn't missing. I just misplaced it or something."

"Think about it, Solie. The key that you don't use was suddenly missing from its proper spot? You only noticed because you were looking for it to give to me. After we used *your* key off *your* key ring to make a copy for me, suddenly the missing key reappears out of nowhere? We brushed it off, but now we know that one of those times he showed up to bring you your mail, he snagged that fucking key. Then used his own copy to come inside and put the key back."

She knew Burt was right. Knew it down to her toes. But denial felt like a safer place, so that's where she decided to hang out just now.

"Uh, okay, Burt. So, why would he show himself a few houses down if he could have just come inside?"

A sweat-inducing image popped into her mind—her bedroom door sliding silently closed this morning. The following chill was so deep, it was as if someone had walked over her grave. What if...? No. No, it couldn't have been. She refused to believe it. Burt was just being paranoid.

"I can't speak to the man's motive, Solie. At all. Maybe the neighbors are right, maybe they're not. But we're not taking any chances. Now, get dressed and let's go see a movie."

"But you have work today. *I* have work today."

"Unless someone is going to die if you don't work today, you are taking the day off. And so am I."

"Fine. But if you're going to make me go see a movie, then I wanna see something with hot men and stuff that goes boom."

"You're on, woman." With a grin, Burt pulled out his mobile, made a quick call and just like that, he'd rescheduled a building walk-through and a design planning session. And none of Solie's clients worked on the weekends so she didn't have to call anyone.

Jogging pants exchanged for a cute skirt and sandals, hand-in-hand, they were out the door for a matinee. And Solie was so happy and comforted she stuffed the weird run-in with *that guy* into a mental sack with all the other shit that had been bugging her. In her head, she set it on fire and threw it off a cliff.

* * * * *

"I never thought I'd like a sequel better than the original but that movie was just…" Two feet into the back den, Solie stopped short, whirled around to the man at her back and scowled. "Burton Khrys, why would you do that?"

"Do what?" he asked, helping her out of her sweater.

"That." She pointed to Mims who had her big furry butt up on one of the loveseats that faced the big bay window and looked out toward the Sound. The shepherd was eating dog food. Out of a can!

"You know she's not allowed on the furniture. And to give her wet food out of a can? That's not even the stuff we feed her."

Annoyed, Solie bore down on her poor dog. She almost felt bad when Mims cowered just a bit. She snatched the can of smelly cheap dog food away and headed to the kitchen to toss it in the trash.

A gentle but firm hand wrapped around her biceps and halted her steps.

"Solie, wait. Call 911. Now."

"What? Why?"

"You asked why I would feed the dog on the couch. But I've been with you since lunchtime yesterday. The only time I left you was to get Dunkin' Donuts super early this morning. When did you see me go buy this funky ass dog food and give it to the dog on the loveseat?"

Oooh, he had a point.

"Call the police, Solie. I'm going to have a look around."

"Okay." Her stomach dropped into her shoes. Oh God. "No problem." This couldn't be happening. The neighbor had told her someone had been coming in and out while she was gone. She didn't want to believe it even though he described her ex. But then again, it could have been any other tall, bald, buff dude, right?

Okay, stop. That thought didn't make it any better.

She headed toward the stairs. She'd call 911, but after she changed into something a bit more comfortable.

She turned the corner to head upstairs…and ran smack into Marcais.

A scream ripped from her throat involuntarily as she scrambled backward.

"What the fuck are you doing in my house?"

She couldn't believe the baffled expression on his face, as if he was the surprised one. So he was off guard, eh? Good. The fucker.

When he didn't answer, Solie moved toward the phone across the living room. "I'm calling the police right now."

"Bitch, you pick up that phone and I swear…"

Solie's heart lodged in her throat when two hundred and fifty pounds of solid muscle stalked her way.

Then Burt was there, standing between her and Marcais.

"Oh, I've been waiting for this," Burt said with the most sinister grin she'd ever seen spread across his beautiful mouth. "Take one more step toward her. Give me an excuse to kick your ass. Any excuse will do."

Marcais might be brave enough to threaten a woman, but he wasn't stupid by any stretch of the imagination. But unfortunately for him, he wasn't that smart either.

He took one step toward Solie.

And in the next instant, he was flat on his back holding his jaw and his nuts.

Burton Khrys did not tolerate threats to a female.

Period.

The police were on the way but unfortunately Marcais had recovered his ability to breathe before they arrived. He scrambled to his feet, backed away, and used his coat sleeve to open the door. Solie just shook her head. What point was there to making sure he had no prints on the door knob when she was looking right at him? Amazing.

And after the police came and took their statements, Burt and Solie went on a little expedition in her house trying to figure out what the hell Marcais was doing up and down the stairs.

What they found had her sitting with tears in her eyes and her mouth wide open. One thing was for sure—she couldn't pretend all was well anymore. Couldn't bask in her own denial. The proof was in her hand.

Cameras. Wireless little cameras.

She'd been under surveillance and hadn't even known it.

The sheriff was already on his way to the base to make the arrest. What the hell else had Marcais done that she was unaware of?

Finally Burt pressed a shot of whisky into her left hand while he took her findings from her right hand and dropped them into a little baggie.

Burt lifted the glass that remained untouched and cool against her fingers. He tipped it up and she obediently drank it as he spoke.

"It's a good thing he's in jail or I'd kick his ass again. But now we know. And better to know what you're dealing with than not."

She emptied the glass and while her gut still burned from that first shot, Burt poured her another. She downed it without hesitation and then let her man take her to bed.

* * * * *

And he knew just what she needed. As angry as she felt over this newest betrayal, what she needed was to feel cherished and loved. And that was something Burt could give her.

"Strip and then put this on," he said, handing her a robe identical to the one she'd worn at Twilight Teahouse on their lunchtime visit to the Japanese Baths. The water is ready. So are the ropes. Are you?"

She looked up and Burton watched her expression morph from sadness and anger to resolve. "Oh God, yes. Always."

"Safe word?" he asked.

Without hesitation, she replied, "Kickass". His woman might be fragile. She might even be broken. But she was not down for the count by any stretch of the imagination.

ALSO BY AUTHOR TJ MICHAELS

Carinian's Seeker, Vampire Council of Ethics Book One
Serati's Flame, Vampire Council of Ethics Book Two
Hatsept Heat, Vampire Council of Ethics Book Three
Seeker's Solace, Vampire Council of Ethics Book Four
Silk Road, Seals of Destiny
Spirit of the Pryde, A Pryde Ranch Shifter Story
Niah's Pride, A Pryde Ranch Shifter Story
Jaguar's Rule
Forever December
Egyptian Voyage
On the Prowl
Entwined Hearts
Shards of Ecstasy
Caramel Kisses
Death and Roses

Anthologies
Mastered: Ten Tales of Sensual Surrender
Doing it the Hard Way
Feral Fascination
Wild Winter

ABOUT THE AUTHOR

TJ is an award-winning author of several romance genres, including paranormal, fantasy, sci-fi and urban fantasy romance. Writing like a madman, TJ hasn't lost steam. Her mind? Yep, that's gone, but steam there is a-plenty. A true Taurus, TJ isn't slowing down and she's definitely too stubborn to stop when she sees the fence!No matter the genre TJ is penning, her favorite thing to do is build worlds. To take you somewhere extraordinary. To transport you to a place where you can close your eyes and slip into your fantasy…

Connect with T.J. at www.TJMichaels.com
and
www.facebook.com/The.Real.TJMichaels